Jessica Steele lives in a friendly Worcestershire village with her super husband, Peter. They are owned by a gorgeous Staffordshire bull terrier called Florence, who is boisterous and manic, but also adorable. It was Peter who first prompted Jessica to try writing and, after the first rejection, encouraged her to keep on trying. Luckily, with the exception of Uruguay, she has so far managed to research inside all the countries in which she has set her books, travelling to places as far apart as Siberia and Egypt. Her thanks go to Peter for his help and encouragement.

Recent titles by the same author:

VACANCY: WIFE OF CONVENIENCE
A PRETEND ENGAGEMENT
HER BOSS'S MARRIAGE AGENDA

A MOST SUITABLE WIFE

BY
JESSICA STEELE

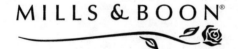

CHAPTER ONE

TAYE let herself back into the apartment and wandered into the sitting room. Looking around at the smart furniture and fittings, she recalled the poky bed-sit she had lived in for most of the three years previously, and knew that she just could not bear to go back to that way of living.

Not only could she not, but, with the rent of this apartment being very much more than she could afford on her own now that Paula had left, Taye determined that she would *not* give up the apartment unless she absolutely had to.

To that end, and after a very great deal of thought, she had just taken the first steps in getting someone to pay half of the rent. She did so hope that someone would see the advert and apply soon.

Unfortunately, because Paula, while giving her the name and address of the letting agent, had taken the lease with her, Taye felt on very rocky ground with regard to her own tenancy agreement. The fact was, although Taye had looked high and low for the lease, she had been unable to find it, and so was unsure of her actual tenancy position.

The lease was in Paula's name and while Paula had said that provided the rent was paid on time—quarterly in advance—she was sure the agents would not care who was living there or who paid the rent, Taye was not so certain.

She would have liked a sight of the lease before Paula

5

had left, if only to have some idea if there was any restriction on sub-letting. Because it seemed to Taye to be fairly obvious that a lease would not be worth as much as the paper it was written on if the tenant went ahead their own merry way.

But she had a feeling that any approach to the agent to check might see Wally, Warner and Quayle saying that there was a 'no flat-share sub-let' clause—and that caused Taye to hesitate to approach them. Yes, she knew that she should approach them. That she ought to go and see them and explain that Paula Neale had left the area. Fear that they might say that she would have to leave too, caused Taye to hold back. Should they be even likely to enquire into her suitability to be a tenant—her financial suitability that was—they would know straight away that by no chance could she pay the high rent required on her own.

Burying her head in the sand it might be but, bearing in mind that she had been Paula's sub-tenant, Taye preferred to look on it from Paula's viewpoint: that as long as the rent was paid they would not care who lived there provided they were respectable and paid the rent when due.

All the same, when considering her options—pay up or leave—Taye knew she did not want to leave and go back to the way she had up until three months ago been living.

Which left the only answer—she must get someone else to pay half the rent the way she had paid half the rent to Paula. And how to go about that? Advertise.

The only problem with that was that Taye felt she could hardly advertise in the paper. Without question she suspected that any agent worthy of the name would keep their eyes on the 'To Let' column of the local paper.

Which meant— Her thoughts were interrupted when someone rapped smartly on the wood panelling of the door. Anticipating it would be one of her neighbouring apartment dwellers, Taye went to answer it.

But, although she thought she had met all of the other tenants in the building in the time she had been there, she would swear she had never caught so much as a glimpse of the tall dark-haired man who stood there before her.

'How did you get in?' she questioned abruptly when for what seemed like ageless seconds the man just stared arrogantly back at her.

She thought she was going to have to whistle for an answer. Then Rex Bagnall, who had a flat on the next floor, rushed by. 'Forget my head...' he said in passing, making it obvious he had just gone out but had dashed back for something he had forgotten—and that answered her question. The man who had knocked at her door had slipped in as Rex had gone out.

Then suddenly it clicked. 'You've come about the flat?' she exclaimed.

For long silent minutes the stern-faced man studied her, and she began to think she was going to have to run for any answer to her questions. But then finally, his tones clipped, 'I have,' he replied.

Oh, grief! She had been thinking in terms of a female to flat-share with! She could not say either that she was very taken with this grim-expressioned mid-thirties-looking man, but she supposed even if she had no intention of renting half the flat to him that there were certain courtesies to be observed.

'That was quick,' she remarked pleasantly. 'I've only just returned from putting the ad in the newsagent's window.' She might have gone on to say that she had been looking for someone of the female gender but Rex Bagnall was back again, dashing along the communal hallway. Not wanting him to hear any of her business, 'Come in,' she invited the unsuccessful candidate.

He followed her into her hall, but so seemed to dominate it that she quickly led the way to the sitting room. She turned, the light was better there, and she observed he was broad-shouldered and casually, if expensively, dressed. He could see her better too, his glance flicking momentarily to her white-blonde hair.

'I—er...' she began, faltered and, began again. 'I know I didn't say so, but I was rather anticipating a female.'

'A female?' he enquired loftily—causing her to wish she knew more about the Sex Discrimination Act and if it came into force in a situation like this.

'Have you shared a flat with a female before?' she asked, feeling a trifle hot under the collar. 'I mean, I don't mean to be personal or anything but...' She hesitated, hoping he would help her out, but clearly he was not going to and she found she was saying, 'Perhaps it won't be suitable for you.'

He looked back at her, unspeaking for a second or two. Then deigned to reply, 'Perhaps I'd better take a look around.'

And such was his air of confidence that, albeit reluctantly, Taye, with the exception of her own bedroom, found she was showing him around the apartment. 'This, obviously, is the sitting room,' she began, and went on to show him the dining room, followed by the bathroom and kitchen and utility room. 'That's my bedroom,' she said, indicating her bedroom door in passing. 'And this is the other bedroom.'

'The one for your—tenant?'

'That's right,' she replied, glad, when he had silently

and without comment inspected everywhere else, to hear him say something at last.

He went into what had been Paula's bedroom and glanced around. Taye left him to it. She returned to the sitting room and was preparing to tell him that she would let him know—it seemed more polite than to straight away tell him, No chance. He was some minutes before he joined her in the sitting room—obviously he had been looking his fill and weighing everything up.

'I see you have a garden,' he remarked, going over to the sitting room window and looking out.

'It's shared by all of us,' she replied. 'The agents send someone to tidy up now and again but it doesn't require too much maintenance. Now, about—'

'Your name?' he cut in. 'I can't go around calling you Mrs de Winter the whole time.'

Her lips twitched. Somehow, when she wasn't sure she even liked the man, his dry comment caught at her sense of humour. He all too plainly was referring to the Mrs de Winter in Daphne du Maurier's *Rebecca*. The Mrs de Winter who all through the book had never been given a first name.

'Taye,' she replied, in the face of his unsmiling look controlling her urge to smile. 'Tayce, actually, but I'm called Taye.' She felt a bit foolish all at once, it suddenly seeming stupid to go on to tell him that her younger brother had not been able to manage Tayce when he had been small, and how Taye had just kind of stuck. 'Taye Trafford,' she completed briefly. Only then did it dawn on her that she should have asked his name the minute he had stepped over the threshold. 'And you are?'

'Magnus—Ashthorpe,' he supplied.

'Well, Mr Ashthorpe—'

'I'll take it,' he butted in decisively.

That took her aback somewhat. 'Oh, I don't think...'

'Naturally there are matters to discuss.' He took over the interview, if interview it be.

Well, it wouldn't hurt to discuss it a little, she supposed. At least she could be civilised. 'Would you like coffee?' she offered.

'Black, no sugar,' he accepted, and she was glad to escape to the kitchen.

No way did she want him for a fellow tenant! No way! Yet, as she busied herself with coffee, cups and saucers, she began to realise that she must not be too hasty here. What if no one else applied? The rent was quite steep after all. Yes, but she might well have a whole horde of people interested in a flat-share. Look how quickly he had seen her ad. That card could not have been in the local newsagent's window above ten minutes, she was sure.

'Coffee!' she announced brightly, taking the tray into the sitting room, setting in down and inviting him to take a seat. She placed a cup and saucer down on the low table near him, and, taking the seat opposite, thought it about time to let him know who was doing the interviewing here. 'The flat—the flat-share—it's for yourself?' she enquired. He stared into her wide blue eyes as though thinking it an odd question. 'I mean—you're not married or anything?' she ploughed on. And when he looked unsmiling back, as if to ask what the devil that had to do with her, 'I only advertised for one person. I wouldn't consider a married couple,' she stated bluntly. She was beginning to regret giving him coffee. She would not mind at all if he left now.

'I'm not married,' he enlightened her.

She looked at him. He was quite good-looking, she observed. No doubt he was more interested in playing the field than in making any long-term commitment. 'This is a fairly quiet building,' she felt she ought to warn him. 'We—um—don't go in for riotous parties.' He took that on board without comment, and she began to wonder why she had bothered mentioning it, because she was growing more and more certain that there was no way she was going to have him as a fellow flat-share. He had not touched his coffee—she could hardly stand up and tell him she would let him know. 'The—er—rent would not be a problem?' she enquired. 'It's paid quarterly— thirteen weeks—and in advance.' From his clothes she would have thought he was used to paying for the best, but she had to talk about something. 'I—er—the landlord prefers the rent to be paid on the old quarter days to fall in line with his quarter-day ground rent payments. He owns the building but not the land on which it's built,' she added, but, conscious that she was talking just for the sake of it, she skidded to an abrupt stop.

Magnus Ashthorpe surveyed her coolly before stating, 'I think I'll be able to scrape my share together.' Which, despite his good clothes, gave her the impression that he was in pretty much the same financial state that she was. Her clothes, limited though they were, were of good quality too.

'Er—what sort of work do you do?' she asked, but as he reached for his coffee she noticed a smear of paint on his index finger: the sort of smudgy mark one got when touching paintwork to see if it was dry.

She saw his eyes follow hers, saw him examine the paint smudge himself. 'I'm an artist,' he revealed, looking across at her.

'Magnus Ashthorpe,' she murmured half to herself. She had never heard of him, but it might embarrass him were she to say so, and she had no wish to hurt his feelings. 'You're—um—quite successful?' she asked instead.

'I get by,' he replied modestly.

'You wouldn't be able to paint here,' she said swiftly, latching on to a tailor-made excuse to turn him down. 'The landlord wouldn't care to—'

'I'm allowed the attic where I'm now living. That serves well as a studio,' Magnus Ashthorpe interrupted her.

'Ah,' she murmured. And, feeling desperate to take charge again, 'Where *are* you living at present?' she asked.

'With a friend,' he answered promptly.

'You're—um…' Heavens, this interviewing business was all uphill. 'You're—er—in a—relationship that— er…' She couldn't finish. By the sound of it he was in a relationship that was falling apart. But she just could not ask about it.

Grey eyes continued to appraise her, but briefly his hard expression seemed to soften marginally, as if he had gleaned something of her sensitivity. But any impression she had of a warmer side to the man was gone in an instant. And his voice was cool when he let her know she could not be more wrong if she thought he would tie himself down to any sort of one-to-one relationship.

'Nick Knight and I have been friends for years. He let me move in a year back, but now he wants to move his girlfriend in.' He shrugged. 'While I prefer not to play gooseberry, Nick prefers to have his spare room back.'

'But you'll continue to work from his attic?'

He nodded, and Taye started to feel better. While she had no intention of offering the flat-share to him, if he had a studio—be it just an attic—then at least he had somewhere he could use as a base if this Nick Knight wanted him to leave sooner rather than later.

Magnus Ashthorpe had finished his coffee, Taye noticed. She got to her feet. 'I'm not awfully sure…' she began, to let him down gently.

'You'll want to see other applicants, of course,' he butted in smoothly.

'Well, I have arranged for the flat-share to be advertised all next week and to include next weekend,' she replied. 'And—um—there will be a question of references,' she brought out from an unthought nowhere.

For answer Magnus Ashthorpe went over to the telephone notepad and in a speedy hand wrote down something and tore the sheet of paper from the pad. 'My mobile number,' he said, handing the paper to her. 'I've also noted the name of my previous landlady. Should you want to take up a reference, I'm sure Mrs Sturgess will be pleased to answer any questions you may have about me.'

Since he was not going to be her co-tenant, Taye did not think she would need the piece of paper, but she took it from him anyhow. 'I'll—um—see you out,' she said, and smiled. It cost nothing and she was unlikely to see him ever again. 'Goodbye,' she said. They shook hands.

She closed the door behind him and went swiftly to the dining room. Standing well back from the window, she saw him emerge from the building. But she need not have worried that he might look up and see her lurking near the dining room window—he was already busy in conversation with someone he had called on his mobile phone. No doubt telling his friend Nick Knight that he had found a place!

Taye went back to the sitting room, the feel of his hand on hers still there. He had a wonderful handshake. Still the same, she knew she would not be phoning this Mrs Sturgess for a reference.

Taye purposely stayed in all of that Saturday and the whole of Sunday, and frequently watched from the dining room window for callers. But callers there were none. She had thought there was a huge demand for accommodation to rent, but apparently no one was interested in renting at such a high rent.

And that was worrying. She had not lived in what was termed the 'garden flat' all that long herself, but already she loved it. She had moved to London three years ago after one gigantic fall-out with her mother. But only now was she in any sort of position to pay half of the rent herself. To find all of the rent would be an impossibility.

Taye had a good job, and was well paid, but she just had to keep something back for those calls from her mother. Despite her mother all but throwing her out, it had not stopped her parent from requiring financial assistance from time to time.

Worriedly, knowing that she did not want to go back to the bed-sit existence she had known before her promotion and pay rise, and prior to Paula Neale's invite to move in and share expenses, Taye thought back to how her life had changed—for the better.

There had always been rows at home—even before her father had decided after one row too many that enough was enough and that they would all be happier, himself included, if he moved out.

His financial ability had made the move viable only when his father had died and he had come into a fund which he had been able to assign during her lifetime to his money-loving wife. The fact that Taye's father had no illusions about her mother's spendthrift ways was borne out by the fact that he had made sure that the fund was paid out to her monthly and not in the lump sum she had demanded.

Taye had been fourteen, her brother Hadleigh five years younger when, nine years ago now, their father had packed his bags and left. She loved him, she missed him, and she had been unhappy to see him go. But perhaps they would all be free of the daily rows and constant carping. Perhaps with him no longer there, the rows would stop.

Wrong! Without her father there for her mother to vent her spleen on, Taye had become her mother's target. Though if being daily harangued by Greta Trafford for some over-exaggerated misdemeanour kept the sharpness of her tongue from Taye's nine-year-old brother, then Taye had supposed she could put up with it. What would happen to Hadleigh, though, when she eventually went off to university Taye had not wanted to dwell on.

Then she had discovered that she need not have worried about it, because when she reached the age of sixteen she discovered that her mother had other plans for her.

'University!' she had exclaimed when Taye had begun talking of staying on at school, and of taking her 'A' levels. 'You can forget that, young lady. You can leave school as soon as you can, get a job and start bringing some money in.'

'But—it's all planned!' Taye remembered protesting.

'I've just unplanned it!' Greta Trafford had snapped viperously.

'But Daddy said…'

'Daddy isn't here! Daddy,' her mother mocked, 'was delighted to shelve his responsibilities. Daddy—'

'But—'

'Don't you interrupt me!' Greta Trafford threatened. 'And you can ''but'' all you want. You're still not going.'

And that Taye had had to accept. But while she had struggled to get over her disappointment and upset at the loss of her dream, she'd known she was going to have to hide how she was feeling from her father. He had been so keen for her to go to university that all she could do was to let him think that she had gone off the idea.

She might have had to accept her mother's assertion that there was no money to spare, but what Taye would not accept was that her father had shelved his responsibilities. He had maybe given up the occupation that had provided them with a very high standard of living, so that his income was nowhere near what it had been. But now working on a farm and living in a tiny cottage that went with the job, his needs small, she knew that in addition to the fund he had assigned for their upkeep, he still sent money to his former home when he could.

It was not enough. Nor was it ever going to be enough. Even when he had been a high earner it had not been enough. Money went through her mother's hands like water. She did not know the meaning of the word thrift. If she saw something she wanted, then nothing would do but that she must have it—regardless of which member of her family ultimately paid.

As bidden, Taye had left school and, having inherited her father's head for figures, she had got a job with a firm of accountants. Her mother had insisted that she hand over her salary to her each month. But by then Taye had started to think for herself. There were things Hadleigh needed for his school work, his school trips, and he was growing faster than they could keep up with. Taye held back as much of her salary as she could get away with, and it was she who kept him kitted out in shoes and any other major essential.

Taye had been ready to leave home years before the

actual crunch came. It was only for the sake of Hadleigh that she had stayed, for he had been a shy, gentle boy.

Taye had reached nineteen and Hadleigh fourteen when Hadleigh, after a row where their mother had gone in for her favourite pastime of deviating from the truth, with the first signs of asserting himself had told Taye, 'You should leave home, Taye.' And when she had shaken her head, 'I'll be all right,' he had assured her. 'And it won't be for much longer. I shall go to university—and I won't come back.'

Perhaps a trace of his words had still been lingering in Taye's head when she journeyed home from work one Friday a year later. She had anticipated that Hadleigh would be grinning from ear to ear at the brand-new bicycle she had saved hard for and had arranged to be delivered on his fifteenth birthday. But she had arrived home to discover her mother had somehow managed to exchange the bicycle she had chosen for a much inferior second-hand one—and had pocketed the difference.

'How *could* you?' Taye had gasped, totally appalled.

'How could I not?' her mother had replied airily. 'The bicycle I got him is perfectly adequate.'

'I wanted him to have something new, something special!' Taye had protested. 'You had no right...'

'No right! Don't you talk to me about rights! What about my rights?'

'It wasn't your money, it was mine. It was dishonest of you to—'

'*Dishonest!*' Her mother's voice had risen an octave— which was always a signal for Taye to back down. Only this time she would not back down. She was incensed at what her money-grubbing mother had done.

So, 'Yes, dishonest,' she had challenged, and it had gone on and on from there, with Taye for once in her life refusing to buckle under the tirade of venom her mother hurled at her.

And, seeing that for the first time she was not going to get the better of her daughter, Greta Trafford had resorted to telling her to follow in her father's footsteps and to pack her bags and leave.

And Taye, like her father, had suddenly had enough. 'I will,' she had retorted, and did. Though it was true she did almost weaken when she went in to say goodbye to Hadleigh. 'Will you be all right?' she asked him.

'You bet,' he said, and gave her a brave grin, and, having witnessed most of the row before he'd disappeared, 'You can't stay. Not now,' he had told her.

Taye had gone to London and had been fortunate to find a room to rent, and more fortunate to soon find a job. A job in finance that she became particularly good at. When her salary improved, she found a better, if still poky, bed-sit.

She had by then written to both Hadleigh and her mother, telling them where she was now living. She also wrote to her father, playing down the row that had seen her leave home. Her mother was the first to reply—the electricity bill was more than she had expected. Since Taye had used some of the electricity—even though she had been at home contributing when she had used it— her mother would be obliged to receive her cheque at her earliest convenience.

Her mother's 'requests' for money continued over the next three years. Which was why—having many times shared a lunch table with Paula Neale in the firm's canteen, and having commented that she would not mind moving from 'bed-sit land'—when Paula one day said she had half a flat to let if she was interested, and mentioned the rent required, instead of leaping at the chance, Taye had to consider it very carefully.

Could she really afford it? Could she not? She was twenty-three, for goodness' sake, Hadleigh coming up to eighteen. And their mother had this time promised he should go to university. Was she to wait until he was at university, Taye wondered, or dared she take the plunge now? It had been late February then, and Hadleigh would go to university in October. Taye—while keeping her fingers crossed that nothing calamitous in the way of unforeseen expenditure was heading her way—plunged.

And here she was now and it was calamitous—though this time that calamity did not stem from her mother but was because, unless she could find someone to share, Taye could see she was in a whole heap of financial trouble. But, so far, no one except for one Magnus Ashthorpe had shown an interest. And, as an interested party, he was the one party she did not want.

All that week Taye hurried home ready to greet the influx of potential flat-share candidates. Julian Coombs, the son of the owner of Julian Coombs Comestibles, where she worked, asked her out, but she declined. She had been out with Julian a few times. He was nice, pleasant and uncomplicated. But she did not want to be absent should anyone see her card in the newsagent's window and call.

But she might just as well have gone out with Julian because each evening she retired to her bed having seen not one single solitary applicant.

She toyed with the idea of inviting Hadleigh to come and stay at the weekend. But he worked most weekends waiting at tables in a smart restaurant about five miles from Pemberton. It was, he said, within easy cycling distance of Pemberton, the village on the outskirts of Hertfordshire where he and their mother lived. And, besides Hadleigh not wishing to miss a chance to earn a little money for himself, Pemberton was not the easiest place to get back to by public transport on a Sunday.

So Taye stayed home and almost took root by the dining room window. Much good did it do. Plenty of people passed by but, apart from other residents in the building, no one came near the door.

And early on Monday evening Taye knew that it was decision time. By now the newsagent would have taken her card out of his window, and she could see no point in advertising again. Clearly the rent required was more than most people wanted to pay. In the nine days since she had placed that card in the newsagent's she had received only one reply. So far as she could see, with the rent due on quarter day in a few weeks' time she had to either give up the apartment—and heaven alone knew what she was going to do if they demanded a quarter's rent in lieu of notice—or she had to consider sharing the flat with a male of the species; a male who, for that matter, she was not even sure she could like.

Oh, she didn't want to leave, she didn't! How could she give up the apartment? It was tranquil here, peaceful here. And with the advantage of the small enclosed garden—a wonderful place to sit out in on warm summer evenings, perhaps with a glass of wine, perhaps chatting to one of her fellow flat dwellers. Perhaps, at weekends, to sit under the old apple tree halfway down the garden. There was a glitzy tinsel Christmassy kind of star lodged in that tree—it had been there, Paula had told her, since January, when a gust of wind had blown it there from who knew where. And Taye loved that too. She was in London, but it felt just like being in the country.

On impulse she went into the kitchen and found the

piece of paper with Magnus Ashthorpe's phone number on it. She should have thrown it away, but with no other applicant in sight she rather supposed it must be meant that she had not scrapped it. Not that she intended to ring him. She would see what sort of a reference this Mrs Sturgess gave him.

'Hello?' answered what sounded like a mature and genteel voice when she had dialled.

'Is that Mrs Sturgess?' Taye enquired.

'Claudia Sturgess speaking,' that lady confirmed.

'Oh, good evening. I'm sorry to bother you,' Taye said in a rush, 'but a man named Magnus Ashthorpe said I might contact you with regard to a reference.'

'Oh, yes, Magnus—er—Ashthorpe,' Claudia Sturgess answered, and suddenly seemed in the best of humours. 'What would you like to know about him?'

'Well, he has applied to rent some accommodation,' Taye replied, it somehow sticking in her throat to confess it was shared accommodation—which she freely admitted was ridiculous. How was she to find out whether or not he was some potential mass murderer if she didn't give the right information and ask the right questions? Giving herself a mental shake, Taye decided she had been reading too many thrillers just lately, and jumped in, 'I wonder how long you have known him and if you consider him trustworthy?'

'Oh, my dear, I've known him for years! Went to school with his mother,' Mrs Sturgess informed her with what sounded like a cross between a giggle and a chuckle. 'May I know your name?' she in turn enquired.

'Taye Trafford.' Taye saw no reason to not tell her. But, hurrying on, 'Do you think he would make a—um—good tenant?'

'First class, Miss Trafford,' Mrs Sturgess replied without the smallest hesitation. 'Or is it Mrs?'

'Miss,' Taye replied. 'You—can vouch for him, then?'

'Absolutely. He's one of the nicest men I know,' she went on glowingly. 'In fact, having had him living with me one time, I'd go as far as to say that if he doesn't get the accommodation you have on offer, I would welcome him back here to live.' Taye reckoned you could not have a better reference than that. 'Where is this accommodation?' Claudia Sturgess wanted to know. 'London?' she guessed.

'Yes,' Taye confirmed. 'He, in your opinion, is trustworthy, then?'

'Totally,' Mrs Sturgess replied, all lightness gone from her tone, her voice at once most sincere. 'He is one of the most trustworthy men I have ever come across. I would trust him with my life.'

'Thank you very much,' Taye said, and, realising that she could not have a better reference than that, she thanked her politely again and put down the phone.

Yet, having been sincerely assured by this woman who had been at school with his mother that Magnus Ashthorpe was totally trustworthy, still Taye hesitated. Even though she knew that mixed flat-shares went on all over the place, she somehow felt reluctant to have him so close. And, if she didn't make that call to him, well, it was not as if he was desperate for somewhere to rent, was it? By the sound of it, Mrs Sturgess, his mother's friend, would have him back living with her like a shot. Presumably, though, he did not want to return there.

Taye thought of her own mother's friend, the hard-bitten Larissa Gilbert. Would she want to go and live with the thin-lipped Larissa? No way.

The decision seemed to be made.

Taye picked up the phone and dialed, half hoping Magnus Ashthorpe had his mobile switched off. He hadn't, but he was already taking a call. She waited a long five minutes and then, aware that she had no option unless she was to go on the apartment-hunting trail her-self—the much smaller apartment hunt; she could not bear the thought of returning to a bed-sit—she had to make that call.

She redialled—it was picked up at the fourth ring. 'Pen…' he began, and then changed it to, 'Hello.'

She guessed his previous caller was probably someone called Penny, and he thought it was she ringing back from his previous call. Sorry to disappoint. 'Hello,' Taye replied, and began to feel more comfortable to know he had got a woman-friend. 'It's Taye Trafford.' He said nothing. Not one solitary word. And she swiftly recalled how he had barely spoken when he had come to view the apartment. Perhaps that was what Mrs Sturgess liked about him—that he was not forever chattering on. 'About the flat-share,' Taye resumed.

'Yes?'

She found his monosyllabic reply annoying and started to have second thoughts. 'There isn't a garage,' she drew out of nowhere, even at the eleventh hour, as it were, attempting, when she really needed him, to put him off. 'Well, there is, but the owner is abroad and has a lot of his belongings stored in it.'

'That won't be a problem.'

'You don't have a car?'

'I find public transport quite useful,' he replied, and, assuming too much in her opinion, 'I'll move in tomor-row,' he announced.

Her mouth fell open in shock. Of all the… 'I'll try to

get off work early—' she began, and was interrupted for her pains.

'You work?' he questioned shortly. 'You have a job?'

She did not care for his tone. 'Of course I have a job!' she exclaimed. They were on the brink of a row—and he hadn't even moved in yet! 'It's how I pay the rent!' she added pithily.

'Huh!' he grunted. It sounded a derogatory grunt to her. But before she could ask him what the Dickens that 'huh' meant, something else struck her.

'You can pay rent in advance?' she queried, everything in her going against asking him for the money but realism having to be faced. 'I shall need the whole quarter's rent before quarter day, the twenty-fourth of June.'

'I'll give you the cash when I see you tomorrow,' he replied crisply.

'A cheque will do as well,' she calmed down a little to inform him—she could bank his cheque on Wednesday, that would still give it plenty of time to clear before quarter day.

'If that's it—' he began.

'One other thing,' she butted in quickly. Again he was silent, and she felt forced to continue. 'Er—naturally I'd expect you to respect my privacy.'

'You mean when you bring your men-friends home?' he questioned tersely. What was it with this man? She had not meant that. Thank goodness there was a lock on the bathroom door. 'Naturally,' he went on when she seemed stumped for an answer, 'you'll afford me the same privacy?'

'When you bring your women-friends back?' she queried tautly.

'Until tomorrow,' he said, and cut the call.

Slowly Taye replaced her telephone. Somehow she just could not see the arrangement working. But, for better or worse, it seemed she had just got herself a tenant.

CHAPTER TWO

MAGNUS ASHTHORPE moved into the garden flat on Tuesday evening. On Wednesday Taye banked the cash he had given her. It exasperated her that he had given her cash. It was almost as if Magnus Ashthorpe did not have a bank account! But, since he seemed to think she would feel happier with the cash than with a cheque, she supposed she should not complain. It was just that thirteen weeks of half the rent in cash was such an awful lot of money to be carrying around.

He had been up and about before her that morning—and she was an early riser. Surprisingly, with the stranger sleeping in the next room, she had slept much better than she had envisaged. She had gone to bed wary and wondering if she should prop a chair under the door handle. Then she recalled the glowing reference Claudia Sturgess had given him, her 'I've known him for years', her 'He's one of the nicest men I know', her comment that she would trust him with her life—and Taye, as it were, bit the bullet, and decided that to place a chair under her bedroom door handle was no way to start out.

By Friday she had started to relax at having a male flat-share. Given that he was rather taciturn of manner, he was quiet and clean. And, apart from the fact that his eyesight appeared a shade faulty when it came to clearing up a few toast crumbs from the work surfaces, Taye felt she had not done too badly to take her one and only applicant. Another point in his favour—he was seldom ever there. He arose early, went out early, and came home late. He was, she decided, one very busy painter.

She frequently worked late herself, but, having accepted a dinner invitation with Julian Coombs that evening, Taye hurried home from her office to shower and change. She found her flat-share had beaten her to it.

For once, having let himself in with the spare keys Paula had left behind, he was home early. Taye could hear the shower running as she went in and walked by the bathroom. It was not a problem; he did not spend anywhere near the length of time in there that Paula had.

Taye went into her bedroom and, Julian having mentioned the smart establishment where they would be dining, extracted a smart dress from her wardrobe. Up until the age of fourteen she had been used to the best of clothes. Habits formed up until the time her father had left home were ingrained deeper than she had known, and she had discovered that she would rather wait until she could afford something with a touch of quality than buy two of something inferior. That was not to say that if a cheaper item looked good, she might not buy it.

She glanced at her watch just as she heard the bathroom door open. Oh, good! Taye left her room in time to see a robe-clad Magnus Ashthorpe leaving the bathroom.

She almost disappeared back into her room but, Get used to it, she instructed herself, he lives here. 'Finished in there?' she asked brightly.

'It's all yours,' he answered, and went to his room, leaving her to it.

A quick shower, a light application of make-up and Taye was seated before her dressing table mirror wondering whether to wear her straight white-blonde hair up or down. Down, she decided. It was Friday night; she had worked hard all week. Time to party.

Well, she qualified, Julian being more earnest than frolicsome, time to unwind. Dressed in a straight dress of heavy silk with fragile shoulder straps, Taye left her room.

To her surprise she found Magnus taking his ease in the sitting room, reading his evening paper. A small 'Oh!' escaped her before she could stop it. He must have heard it because, unspeaking, he lowered his paper, and she somehow felt obliged to explain, 'I didn't expect you to still be here.'

'Here is where I live,' he reminded her coolly, and while she felt a touch embarrassed, and a touch annoyed at one and the same time, she saw his glance skim over her silky shoulders, bare apart from the thin straps of her dress, down over her slender but curving in the right places form, then dropping to what Paula had called her 'glorious legs'. Clearly, though, he was not impressed by what he saw, because his expression seemed to tighten when bluntly he challenged, 'You have a date?'

Any embarrassment she had felt disappeared as her annoyance surged. As if it had anything to do with him if she had a date or not!

But this was no way to go on. She was stuck with him until the end of September at least. With difficulty she swallowed down her ire, her glance flicking over his fresh shirt and lounge suit. 'You don't actually appear dressed for staying in,' she replied. She smiled. He stared at her upturned mouth, his gaze lingering for a second before suddenly his grey eyes moved up to her lovely blue eyes. His eyes hardened; he did not smile.

With no idea what to make of him she went into the kitchen to wait until Julian called. She knew quite a few men whom she thought she could regard as friends. They were an eclectic mix at Julian Coombs Comestibles and she got on well with all of them. But this man, this Magnus Ashthorpe, was something else again! He might be totally trustworthy, and Claudia Sturgess might think he would make a first-class tenant but, Taye owned, changing her mind about not having done too badly to have him as a fellow tenant, right now she was finding him extremely hard work.

Thankfully Julian arrived ten minutes before the appointed time, so she did not have to hang about in the kitchen over-long. She went to the intercom to check that it was Julian ringing the bell, and while releasing the outer door catch she turned to her flat-share and civilly informed him that she did not think she would be late.

Like he cared! He looked unblinking back at her. And suddenly she was remembering their conversation about privacy. 'Er—will you be bringing anyone back?' she enquired nicely—like *she* cared!

For a moment she thought he was going to let her whistle for an answer. But then, dryly, he replied, 'We'll go to hers.'

Her lips twitched. What was it about this man? He had not intended to amuse her with his 'go to hers' but, when she did not particularly like him half of the time, he seemed to have the oddest ability to make her want to laugh.

Julian tapping lightly on the door did away with any further speculation. She went and let him in and, as a courtesy—one of them should make an effort to make this flat-share work—she took Julian into the sitting room and introduced him to Magnus.

It pleased her to discover that there was nothing wrong with Magnus's manners when there was a third person present. He shook hands with Julian and in the few minutes before she and Julian went out to Julian's car exchanged politenesses and showed that he was not lacking when it came to social graces.

'I imagined your new flat-mate to be somewhere in his early twenties,' Julian opined as they drove along. 'He— Magnus—he's quite sophisticated, isn't he? You know, he's got that sort of confident air about him.'

'I suppose he has. I've not really thought about it.'

'You're getting along all right?' Julian asked.

Taye wasn't truly sure that they were 'getting along all right', but diplomatically replied, 'I don't see very much of him. I think he has a date tonight, so I may not see him again before morning.' And probably not then if he stays out all night up to no good at 'hers'.

'Her' was probably Pen—Penelope, Penny—Taye mused, and then forgot about the pair of them, or tried to, as she gave herself over to enjoying her evening. Julian was three years older than her. He was pleasant and charming, good, undemanding company, and she liked him very much. He was easy to get along with and seemed to agree with everything she said.

So much so that, when she caught herself thinking that she would not mind too much hearing if he had an opposing view, she began to wonder for one panicky moment if she had inherited some of her mother's traits and would turn into some cantankerous woman who liked to argue purely for the sake of it.

Taye felt better when she thought of the many times her mother had thrown at her that, while she had inherited Greta Trafford's beauty—her mother's words, not Taye's—she had inherited nothing else of her but was in temperament totally her father's daughter.

'Shall we have coffee here?' Julian asked. 'Or we

could go back to my place? I make a splendid cup of coffee.'

Julian had a flat about fifteen minutes away from where she lived. And Taye had once been back to his flat for coffee. They had kissed a little, she recalled, and it had been quite enjoyable getting some practice in. But she never had been too free with her kisses and, while finding Julian physically attractive, he was not so attractive that she lost sight of what was right for her. To make love with him had not been right then. Who knew? It might be at some future date. But for now that time had not arrived.

'Coffee here, shall we? Do you mind?'

'Yes, I mind,' Julian replied, but, as ever the nice person he truly was, 'But anything you say,' he added, and grinned.

Most oddly, though, she did not feel like asking him in when he stopped his car outside her building. 'I won't ask you in,' she said, adding quickly for an excuse, 'Magnus may have changed his mind and decided to do a bit of—er—entertaining at home, and until I get to know him better I shouldn't like to embarrass him.' The idea that arrogant Magnus Ashthorpe would ever be embarrassed about anything was laughable, but Julian accepted her excuse.

'Come out with me tomorrow?' he asked. 'We could…'

'I'd rather planned to visit my father tomorrow,' she found she was inventing on the spot.

Julian swallowed any disappointment. 'He lives in Warwickshire, doesn't he? I think I remember you mentioning it one time. I'll drive you down, if you like?'

'I couldn't let you,' she answered quickly. 'It will be no trouble for my father to pick me up from the station.

I'd better go in,' she said in a rush—and just had to wonder what had got into her that, when she quite enjoyed Julian's company, she should put him off. And why when, as they left the car and he walked to the outer door with her, he went to take her in his arms, as he had a few times before, she should experience a feeling of not wanting to be kissed.

And what was even more odd was that an image of Magnus Ashthorpe should at that moment spring to mind. 'Goodnight, Julian. I've had a lovely time,' she said.

And, mentally sticking her tongue out at that Magnus Ashthorpe image, she stretched up and kissed Julian— though quickly pulled back when she felt his arms begin to tighten about her. He let her go and she went indoors, still pondering what was going on in her psyche.

To her surprise there was a light on in the sitting room when she went in. 'I didn't expect to see you back,' she recovered to say pleasantly to Magnus, who used the remote and switched off the television. 'Don't do that on my account,' she hurriedly bade him.

'It had just finished. Have a good time?' he thought to ask. She liked him better like this.

'Julian's excellent company. I'm about to make a drink. Would you like one?' Perhaps they could set about creating some kind of flat-sharing harmony, some flat-sharing give and take.

'Thank you,' he accepted, but followed her into the kitchen.

'Did you have a nice time?' she kept up the politeness to enquire.

'So-so,' he replied, and Taye suspected Penny was on her way out. Her lips twitched at the touch of whimsy that came to her that the Penny was about to be dropped.

'Thoughts of Julian make you smile?' Magnus interrupted her trend—and suddenly he sounded quite grim.

'I told you—he's very good company,' she reminded him. Grief, this man was never the same two minutes together!

'I seem to know his name from somewhere?'

'You've probably heard of his father—Julian Coombs of Julian Coombs Comestibles. They're big in—'

'I know them,' he cut in. 'Quite financially sound, from what I hear.'

She did not know how he, an artist, got to hear these things, but, working quite high up with the Finance Director, she knew that Magnus had heard quite rightly. 'They're flourishing,' she agreed.

Magnus looked at her speculatively for long moments. 'So the son isn't exactly on his uppers?' he commented at last.

And Taye at once resented the inference she saw in his comment; as if he considered she would not be going out with Julian were he not loaded. 'Julian will one day inherit a fortune,' she said stiffly, in the interests of compatibility doing her best not to fall out with the man facing her.

'And you're serious about him?'

Taye felt her hackles rising. She had near enough had it with one Magnus Ashthorpe, and no way was she ready to discuss her love life with him, thank you very much! 'I might be!' she retorted, her fine blue eyes flashing.

Hard grey eyes looked hostilely back. Then at that moment the kettle snicked off. 'Forget the drink!' he ordered curtly, and, turning about, left her staring blankly after him. Just what had that been all about?

By morning, trying not to think of the longest three months of her life stretching out in front of her, Taye resolved once again to do her best to get some sort of amicability going. To that end, up early and in the kitchen before him, she overcame the thought that if he wanted a drink he could jolly well make it himself.

'Coffee?' she offered when he joined her, having only just made a fresh pot.

'Thanks,' he accepted. No smile, just a hard stare. And, as if taking up from where they had left it last night, 'How long have you known Julian Junior?' he questioned, not the smallest sign of humour in his expression.

Julian Junior! Taye's decision to try and get some amicability going began to flounder. She could have mentioned that she and Julian worked at the same place, but did not feel inclined to do so. Though she did give herself top marks that she answered Magnus Ashthorpe at all. 'Ages,' she replied briefly—and received another of his hard-eyed looks. Resisting the temptation to slam his coffee down on the counter top next to him, Taye controlled her spurt of annoyance and informed him evenly, 'I shall be away overnight. I'm—'

'Julian Coombs?' he barked before she could finish.

To the devil with him. This kitchen just was not big enough for the two of them. Carefully she placed his mug of coffee down near him. 'Actually, no,' she replied with hard-won control. 'Not Julian. His name is Alden. He's—'

But, making cutting her off mid-speech into an art form, Magnus Ashthorpe did it again. 'Just how many lovers do you run at one and the same time?' he snarled.

This time it was she who went without her drink. 'That's none of your business!' she erupted hotly—and got out of there before she gave in to the temptation to hit him.

She was on Paddington railway station before she had cooled down sufficiently to be able to think of something other than the abrasive manner of her flat-share. Oh, why did he have to be the only one to reply to her advert? Just about anyone else would have been preferable.

Taye pushed thoughts of Magnus Ashthorpe out of her mind and took out her phone and rang her father. 'Hello, it's me, Taye,' she said when he answered.

'Hello, love. I was just thinking about you,' he said, and she could hear the smile in his voice. 'Any chance of you coming to see me some time soon? I—er—need to see you about—something.'

She felt pleased that her father wanted to see her, but was intrigued about the 'something' he needed to see her about. 'As it happens, I'm on Paddington Station as we speak,' she answered with a smile.

'Great!' he said enthusiastically. 'I'll pick you up in Leamington. Eleven o'clock?'

Her father was on the platform waiting for her when her train pulled in. And Taye, having searched and wondered and speculated all through the train journey to Royal Leamington Spa, was utterly flabbergasted when, not waiting until they arrived at his cottage, he revealed what that 'something' was.

Though she supposed she rather invited it when, as they got into his ramshackle car, she more or less straight away asked, 'You needed to see me about something?'

'If you hadn't managed to come here, I was going to try to come to you.' And, straight on the heels of that, after only the smallest hesitation, 'I've met someone,' he announced as in his ancient car they trundled out of town and towards a rural area.

'You've met someone?' Taye asked, not with him for the moment. Then, as it began to sink in, 'A girl? I mean, a woman?'

'Hilary's forty-seven,' Alden Trafford replied. 'Do you mind, Taye?'

Taye was more winded than minding. 'But... No,' she said then. 'Just give me a minute to...' Her voice tailed away. She turned to give him a sideways look. He was fifty-one and, given that he was virtually penniless—her mother would see to that—quite an attractive man. 'Er— is it serious?' Taye asked, getting her head back together.

'I'm going to ask your mother for a divorce,' he re- plied, and Taye reckoned he could not get much more serious than that. Her mother would create blue murder!

'Oh, dear,' Taye murmured faintly.

'I'm sorry, Taye. Unfortunately you'll not be able to get through this without some of your mother's bitterness spilling over onto you in some way. But you're living away from home now, and it won't be all that long before Hadleigh goes off to university. And, while I want to be fair to you both, I want to be fair to Hilary too.'

'Of course. Don't worry about us. Um—have you known—Hilary—long?'

'Three years. But it's only since New Year—we were both at a friend's house—that things have—er—hmm— blossomed between us,' he answered, with an embar- rassed kind of cough. 'Anyhow, I want to marry her, and your mother and I have been separated long enough now to make a divorce between us a quite simple procedure.'

Taye smiled; what else could she do? The divorce might be a simple formality, but the fall-out it engendered would not be.

'Will I meet Hilary this weekend?' she asked.

'I rang her after your call. I asked her to pop round this afternoon and have a cup of tea with us.'

Taye took to Hilary within a very short time of meeting her. Hilary was a widow, worked as a schoolteacher, was short and a little on the plump side—and it was obvious from the way Alden Trafford's face lit up when he saw her that this woman meant everything to him.

And, as Taye adjusted to this new state of affairs, she could only be glad for him. He had had it tough for long enough. Prior to him leaving their home he had worked in high finance. But, feeling stale in the work he had been doing, he had changed employers—but had not cared for some of their accounting procedures. When he had started asking pertinent questions he had found himself out of a job. He had been unable to find other work and, after a year during which his savings had dwindled, his wife had seemed to much prefer her room to his company—and then his father had died—and he had moved out.

When Taye returned to London early on Sunday evening it was not without a few worries gnawing away at her. That she had taken to Hilary Wyatt caused Taye to feel a little disloyal to her mother. But there was no denying that she and Hilary had liked each other. And, seeing how much Hilary meant to her father and soon realising that he wanted to spend as much time as he could with the woman he hoped to make his wife, Taye had invited her to stay on to dinner.

They were suited, her father and Hilary, but all hell was going to break loose when her mother heard about it. After thinking about it, Taye's father had decided he would do his present wife the courtesy of telling her in person. In his view, though he considered he owed her very little, it did not seem right to let her find out via the auspices of his lawyer.

Taye let herself into the apartment she now shared with Magnus Ashthorpe, and saw he was speaking with someone on his mobile phone. 'I'll come over next week,' he was saying warmly. 'No, no.' He was obviously answering something said on the other end.

Taye decided to take her overnight bag into her bedroom and so leave Magnus to finish his call in private—although for that matter he was quite capable of walking to his own bedroom and taking his phone with him.

Taye had reached her bedroom door when, 'Leave it with me, Elspeth,' she heard him say. 'I'll deal with it.'

So, Pen-Penny was out? Goodbye, Penelope—hello, Elspeth!

When she thought she had given him enough time to finish his call, though to be on the safe side Taye opened her bedroom door a crack and listened, she left her room. Soon, she suspicioned, when her mother knew about the divorce, there would be enough unpleasantness around without inviting more from anywhere else.

That being so, she decided to ignore the spat she'd had with Magnus yesterday morning. Pinning a pleasant look on her face, she popped her head around the sitting room door. 'I'm making a pot of tea if you're interested?'

'Thanks,' he accepted, and buried his head in his newspaper.

Waitress service! Now, now, don't get cranky. She made the tea and took it through to the other room. He lowered his paper as she poured some tea and placed his down on the small table next to him.

'Good weekend?' she enquired, attempting to build bridges.

'Average,' he replied. 'You?'

She thought about it. Yes, given that she had been a touch shaken by her father's news, it had been a good weekend, a happy weekend. 'Lovely,' she replied, a smile in her eyes as she thought about it.

'Hmph!' Magnus grunted sourly, causing her to want

to give up. The man was insufferable! 'And does dear Julian know about dear Alden?' he had the nerve to ask.

Does dear Penelope know about dear Elspeth? From somewhere Taye found a smile. 'Well, they've never actually met,' she replied, keeping her tone as pleasant as she could in the circumstances. 'But Julian did very kindly offer to save me a train journey and drive me to meet him.'

'My stars, there's no end to your brass-necked—'

Taye, having roused him to anger—without any idea why—found tremendous delight in cutting in on what he was saying for a change. 'Naturally I refused—'

Her delight was short lived. 'Even you baulked at entertaining two lovers at one and the same time!' He cut her off aggressively—and insultingly.

She'd had it with him! Oh, how she'd had it with him! 'For your information,' she hissed furiously, 'Alden Trafford is my father!' And, unable to bear being in the same room with this unbearable man any longer, she sprang up from her chair, tears of she knew not what— anger, hurt—spurting to her eyes. She made it as far as the sitting room door before he caught up with her, and with a hand on her left arm he halted her and turned her round to face him.

He looked down into her shining mutinous eyes. Taye looked belligerently back at him. 'Oh, hell!' he muttered, his hand dropping away from her.

'If that was an apology, I don't think much of it!' she snapped, and, feeling better now that the threat of tears had subsided, 'You're an insulting, insufferable, diabolical pig!' she laid into him. 'And if it wasn't for the fact that I've got your rent and that no one else has applied, I'd kick you out right now!'

He stared at her. And then he laughed. To her astonishment, he actually laughed! His lips parted, showing a superb set of teeth, and his head tilted back and he gave a short bark of laughter.

Rebelliously she continued to look hostilely at him. Then all at once she started to see the funny side of it too. She was five feet nine, and slender with it. He was well over six feet, broad-shouldered and with plenty of muscle. The idea of physically setting about kicking him out *was* laughable. 'Well,' she mumbled lamely, but could not control that, when she had been absolutely furious with him, she could not now stop her mouth from picking up at the corners.

'Come and finish your tea,' he persuaded, 'and tell me all about your weekend.'

Persuaded was the right word. Because, when she was determined cats and dogs would sprout feathers before she would sit sipping tea with him again, she found she was returning with him to take the chair she had so rapidly bolted from.

Though to her mind, as he went and took the seat opposite, there was very little of her time spent with her father that she wanted to tell him about. The fact that her father wanted a divorce from her mother was something that had to be conveyed to her mother before it became general knowledge.

'You had a lovely time, you said?' Magnus prompted. 'What did you do?'

'Not very much. It was just lovely being with him, relaxing. You know, generally unwinding.'

'Where do your parents live?'

Taye, a rather private person when she thought about it, could see no harm in him knowing a little of her family. 'My mother lives on the outskirts of Hertfordshire, my father in Warwickshire.'

'Your parents are divorced?'

Not yet! 'Separated,' she supplied, and, feeling she was being ever so slightly grilled here, was about to ask him about his parents when he picked up from that one word that matters were far from amicable with her parents.

'And never the twain shall meet?'

'Something like that,' she murmured. But, to her astonishment, heard herself confiding, 'Though I think my father intends to call on my mother fairly soon.'

'He wants a reconciliation?'

Like blazes! Her parents may have been close at one time, but they were poles apart now, and both liking it that way. Taye shook her head, her lips sealed. 'How about your parents?'

Abruptly any sign of good humour left him. 'What about them?' he asked shortly.

And she was just a little bit fed up with Mr Blow Hot, Blow Cold Magnus Ashthorpe. Though tenacious if nothing else, and always believing that fair was fair and she had after all told him about her parents, 'Are they still married?' she asked. 'I take it they were married?' she asked sweetly.

He didn't think that funny, she observed, as a sudden glint came into his eyes. 'My father was killed in an accident when I was fifteen.'

'I'm sorry.' The apology had come instinctively. 'Have you any brothers or sisters?' she enquired gently—and wondered as his expression hardened what she had done now.

'That's none of your business!' he retorted bluntly.

Taye stood up and this time he did nothing to prevent her from leaving. 'I made the tea,' she said pointedly. 'It wouldn't hurt you to wash the cups and saucers.' With that she put her nose in the air and stormed out. It wasn't a brilliant exit line, but it was the best she could think of on the spur of the moment.

Thankfully she saw little of him the next day. And on Tuesday she woke up and made herself think not long now before she got rid of him. From where she was viewing it, though, July and August, not to mention September, were going to stretch out endlessly.

She worked late on Wednesday, but found, Magnus home before her, that there was a mild thawing of hostilities in that, making tea for himself, he actually offered her a cup. 'Good day at work?' he enquired when, choosing to drink her tea in the kitchen, she pulled out a chair and he followed suit.

'Not bad,' she answered, not trusting him—he was as changeable as the wind.

'Where do you work?' he wanted to know. He had been living under the same roof for a week and only now he wanted to make overtures of friendship? He could take a running jump.

'Julian Coombs Comestibles,' she answered briefly.

'Which is where you met Julian Coombs Junior?'

Again Taye had an uncanny feeling that she was being given the third degree. But she'd had some of this merchant before, with his draw-her-out tactics and then, when she started asking questions in return, slapping her down.

'True,' she answered warily.

'How long have you been going out with him?' Magnus asked crisply.

She expected the big freeze any moment now. 'Long enough,' she replied.

He let that pass, but, 'What do you do there—at Coombs Comestibles?' he wanted to know.

He could not possibly be interested. But, perhaps *he* wanted to build a few bridges this time. She gave him the benefit of the doubt. 'I work for the Finance Director,' she conceded a little.

'You're an accountant?'

She shook her head. 'I don't have any qualifications. I just sort of seem to have a head that's happy absorbing numbers,' she answered modestly, aware that she was quite well thought of at Julian Coombs Comestibles. 'I seem to have inherited my father's aptitude for figure work,' she expanded, then decided, for all Magnus Ashthorpe appeared to look interested, that she had said quite sufficient.

'Your father's a mathematician?'

'He did at one time work in the upper echelons of complicated calculations, but he's a farm hand now,' she replied. 'Though he still keeps his hand in with accountancy,' she added, and explained, 'Only last weekend he was saying how he'd taken a look at his employer's figure-work to help out, and now seems to be doing more paperwork than anything else.'

'And he's happy with that?'

Taye thought back to last weekend. She had never seen him look more contented. 'Oh, yes,' she said. But, getting to her feet, 'And now I'd better dash. Julian's picking me up in half an hour.'

She looked at Magnus, mentally daring him to make some snide remark about her 'lover'. And it was true, he did look as though he was about to lob some acid remark her way.

She braced herself. But when it came, it was a dry, 'I'll see to the cups and saucers, then, shall I?'

Taye left him, only just holding down a laugh. She reached her room and discovered she was smiling anyway. What was it about the man? Never, ever had she come across such a one. He could make her angry, furious, bring her to the brink of tears and, in a split second, he could make her want to laugh.

What it was she could not tell, and in the end she gave up trying to puzzle it out and started to get ready to go for a light meal with Julian. There was a new pizza parlour he had heard of and thought they might like to give it a try.

Taye left her office at the end of her working week knowing that she should go to Pemberton and see her brother and mother. The thing was, though, that she had an idea that her father was planning to make the trip to Pemberton this weekend. And, on balance, Taye thought she would not be doing her father any favours by being there. She knew in advance that he was in for an uncomfortable time, and such was his sensitivity he would by far prefer that she was not around as a witness.

Which meant, of course, that she would really have to make that visit the following weekend. It would not be a very pleasant weekend; she knew that in advance too. All she could hope was that in the days between her father's visit and her own her mother would have had time to cool down.

Magnus was first home. It was the greyish sort of day that sometimes happened in June. Taye suspected the light in his attic studio must have defeated him. Artists needed plenty of good light—didn't they?

He was in the shower. She saw no harm in making them both a cup of tea while she waited. She dropped her bag and bits of shopping down and had just set the kettle to boil when a phone rang. It was not her phone. She looked about and saw Magnus's phone on one of the work surfaces. She went over and looked down at it.

'Elspeth' she read, and as Taye saw it she had two—no, three choices. She could take the phone to the bathroom to him. No, thank you. She could ignore it. Or she could answer it. Oh, he'd just love that wouldn't he? Her having a cosy chat with his girlfriend!

Taye chose the middle option and ignored it, and, changing her mind about tea, went to get out of her office clothes. Wearing a light satin kimono, her father's Christmas gift, she got out the trousers and top she intended to wear for her date with Julian that night. She pinned her hair up so it shouldn't get soaked in the shower, and then heard the bathroom door open.

Believing she had given Magnus time to get clear, she left her room—and met him, robe clad. His hair was pushed back, damp and black, and she glanced down and found she was thinking what nice legs he had. Then all at once she was so tongue-tied by the idiocy of that thought that she could not think to say good evening. She switched her gaze abruptly upwards. Magnus was not saying anything either, but seemed taken by her white-blonde hair all bundled up any old how on top of her head.

Then his faintly amused grey eyes had transferred to her blue eyes, and, not liking to be an object of fun, Taye found her voice and blurted out, 'Elspeth rang.'

My word, had she said the wrong thing! On the instant his expression darkened. 'You spoke to her?' he grated, outraged in a moment. 'You answered my phone!' he snarled. 'You—'

Taye was not far behind when it came to instant fury. 'Would I dare?' She cut through what he was about to say. 'It lit up!' she hurled at him. 'And I can read!'

With that, she pushed past him and went fuming into the bathroom. My heavens, what a man! He was a monster! Thank goodness she had a whole three months in which to take her time and find herself a more congenial flat-mate. Oh, she could hardly wait to give Magnus Ashthorpe his marching orders!

Taye fastened her thoughts on that and started to feel better suddenly—she did so look forward to telling him goodbye. In fact she had never looked forward to anything so much. Oh, what pleasure, oh what joy. She did not know how she would be able to wait to wish him good riddance as she slammed the door shut after him!

CHAPTER THREE

WHEN Taye left for her office on the following Monday, the end of the June to September quarter seemed to be light years away. They were, as usual, busy in her department, which meant that she worked late. That did not particularly bother her. She had nothing she wanted to rush home for. She had made the decision to not try to be friendly with Magnus Ashthorpe any more. What was the point? It always ended up with them snapping and snarling away at each other. It reminded her of being back in her old home in Pemberton with all that bad feeling—no wonder her father had left home!

Her sense of humour came along and tripped her up at that point. She wasn't married to the wretched man. And whoever it was who would eventually marry Magnus Ashthorpe, she was more than welcome to him. She wouldn't take him on for a gold-lined pension!

Taye arrived at her building and let herself in through the main outer door, checked the post table in the hall as she passed—nothing for her—and mentally prepared herself to do battle with *him* if he was in one of his sour moods. But, with any luck, the object of her non-affections would be out.

Squaring her shoulders in case, she inserted her key in the apartment door and went in from the hall into the sitting room—and had the shock of her life! For there, a coffee and a plate of sandwiches in from of him, sat her brother! And sitting opposite was a relaxed looking Magnus Ashthorpe.

47

'Hadleigh!' she gasped, as he left his chair and came over to greet her. 'What are you doing here?'

Her surprises for the day were apparently not over. 'Magnus let me in,' he answered. 'And when time went on and we didn't know what time you'd be home, Magnus made me some sandwiches.'

'You…' She turned to her loathsome flat-share, her mouth falling open in shock. 'Er—thank you, Magnus,' she managed, her thoughts flying in every direction. What was Hadleigh doing here? And what had he and Magnus been talking about? 'Well, I'm always pleased to see you, Hadleigh,' she told him, urging him to sit down and finish his sandwiches. *Magnus* had made them for him!

She took a close inspection of her brother and from what she knew of him thought, from the look of strain in his eyes, the uptight look of him, that something was badly amiss. Had Magnus spotted that too? Had he actually, on learning Hadleigh was her brother, by inviting him in and sitting him down, thought to help him through whatever was troubling him? But that was not the Magnus she knew. Or, remembering his 'Oh, hell' when he must have spotted she was on the brink of tears that time—his fault, of course—was he more sensitive than she had given him credit for?

But there was no time to go into that now, time only, without giving away family confidences, to find out what was upsetting her brother. 'Does Mother know you've popped up to see me?' she asked casually, knowing full well that whatever it was that troubled him, her mother's hand would be in it somewhere.

'Nope!' Hadleigh answered tautly, and Taye wished Magnus would make himself scarce so that she could have a private talk with Hadleigh.

But, was he moving? Was he blazes! She started to

feel annoyed with him, then wondered how she could feel that way when he, observing her brother was all tension, had endeavoured to get him to unwind.

'I'll just go and make myself a drink then we can have a chat,' she said, with a smile to her brother and a big hint to Magnus Ashthorpe.

Much good did it do her! He continued to sit there. And, while she was more interested in talking to Hadleigh than in making a drink, she was left having to go into the kitchen and leaving Magnus there with him.

For a further surprise, however, she had barely switched the kettle on when Magnus followed her in. 'I'll do that,' he volunteered, and she was so taken aback that she forgot entirely about Hadleigh for a moment.

'You will?' she replied faintly.

'That's one very stewed up young man in there—I think he needs his big sister's support until he gets himself more together.'

She stared at Magnus and admitted she had never suspected this sensitive, more intuitive side in him. 'Has he—er—said—anything to you?'

Magnus gave her a sardonic look that was more in keeping with the man she thought she knew. 'He hasn't let any family skeletons out of the cupboard if that's what you're asking. Though he did mention that your father had paid a visit yesterday. But you told me yourself that he intended to call on your mother.' Magnus paused. 'Has your father's visit anything to do with it, do you suppose?'

Taye gave a small sigh. 'Just about everything, I imagine.' And, having said that much, 'My father told me last Saturday that he intends to divorce my mother. He would have called yesterday to acquaint her with his intention.'

Magnus studied her for a few moments. 'It upsets you that your parents are divorcing?'

'I'm more concerned about my brother,' Taye replied, and left Magnus to return to the sitting room. Not sure how much private time she had before Magnus joined them, 'How's Mother?' she asked for starters.

'I'm not going back,' he said mulishly. Which answered her question precisely. Her mother was in fine shrewish form, and Hadleigh was getting the backlash from their father's visit. 'Dad came yesterday,' Hadleigh went on. 'He wants a divorce—and she's playing all hell!'

Hadleigh was usually much more respectful when speaking of his mother, so Taye could only guess that their mother had gone all the way over the top this time. 'Are you upset that Dad's getting a divorce?' Taye asked gently.

'He should have divorced her years ago!' Hadleigh sniffed. 'I'm not going back. I'm not,' he repeated.

Taye had to make a hurried decision. 'You don't have to.' Not tonight at any rate. 'I can make you a bed up on the sofa.'

'Did you know? About the divorce?'

'I popped down to see Dad last weekend,' Taye admitted.

'He's got a lady-friend,' Hadleigh stated. 'Mother went ape! If it was me I wouldn't have told her, but you know Dad. Tell the truth and shame the devil.'

'I'd better give her a ring and let her know where you are.'

'Huh! You think she'll be worried about me?' Hadleigh asked cynically, and Taye could not believe this change in her sweet and shy brother! Not until, that was, he added in a still shocked voice, 'She was positively gloating when she told me I could forget all about university. That she was cancelling everything and that I could go and get myself a full-time job, starting as of now.'

Taye stared at him in disbelief. Then she started to get angry. Her mother had determined that *she* could not go to university, thereby robbing her of her chance; she was *not* going to do the same with Hadleigh.

But, in the face of him being so upset—and she could quite see why—Taye saw no point in distressing him further by going into a rant. 'She didn't mean it.' She tried to soothe him down. 'She was upset at—'

'She meant it.'

'I'll ring—' Taye began, about to say she would ring her immediate boss—there being nothing for it but that she would take a day off work tomorrow and go back with him.

'I'm not going back,' he said stubbornly. And, while Taye was thinking, We'll see... 'I like Magnus, by the way. Are you and he—er—an item?'

'No. Good heavens, no. We just go halves on the rent, that's all.' Her brother liked him—but then Hadleigh was still in shock! 'I'd better go and see where my coffee's got to,' she said, realising that since Magnus *was* paying half the rent she had better have a word with him about her brother staying the night. Hadleigh had endured enough, with all his thoughts, hopes and dreams of university disappearing, without any more tension being created if Magnus objected to him staying.

Magnus was still in the kitchen when she went in. 'Found out what the problem is?' he enquired, and she realised he had deliberately stayed out of the way.

She nodded, but did not elucidate. 'The thing is, Pemberton—the village where Hadleigh lives—is a

Dickens of a place to get to by public transport most times, more especially weekends, and…' with a glance to her watch '…at this time of night.' She paused for breath. 'Have you any objection if he sleeps on the sofa here tonight?'

'He's a tall lad.'

'It's a three- or four-seater.'

'Finished your chat?'

'For the moment,' Taye replied.

'How old is he?'

She did not know what that had to do with anything. 'Eighteen—just,' she answered, trying to keep up with this man's brain.

And still hadn't caught up when, 'Then we won't be breaking any licensing laws,' he stated. She blinked, and received another surprise, not to say shock, when Magnus added, 'That young man's wound up so tight he's going to fracture at any minute. All right with you if I take him for a pint?'

Her head jerked back and Taye could only look at the tall dark-haired Magnus in astonishment. What was more likely to have Hadleigh unwinding, as young as he was, than a beer in some pub?

'Oh, Magnus,' she said shakily. But, suddenly recalling how easily he could turn, 'You won't get all—stroppy—over nothing with him, will you?'

For a minute, as a hard light entered his eyes, she thought he was going to revert to the sour brute she was more familiar with. But whatever thoughts had come to him, he for once overcame them. 'I give you my word—I'll save all my spleen only for you,' he promised nicely.

Hadleigh, who in his weekend job as a waiter had downed the odd pint or two after his work, was all for the idea of going to some bar with Magnus. Taye waited until they had gone and then rang her mother's number.

Greta Trafford was not home, though Taye knew in advance that she was not out looking for Hadleigh. When the answer machine kicked in, Taye said, 'Hello. It's Taye. Hadleigh's with me.' She debated briefly about telling her she would be coming with him tomorrow when he returned, but decided to leave it at that. Then she went to turn the sofa into a bed.

Taye could not get to sleep that night for thinking about everything. Even knowing her mother as she did, she could barely credit that she could be this mean. Particularly as she had known that Hadleigh, from a very young age, had been way above average intelligence, his recent school work classed as academically outstanding.

Knowing that the more she thought about it the more het up she was becoming—not conducive to sleep—Taye channelled her thoughts elsewhere. And what about Magnus, her brute of a flat-share? His behaviour that evening had been faultless! Albeit he had promised to save all his spleen only for her, he had behaved impeccably the whole time Hadleigh had been around. He had even made him some sandwiches too!

They had not stayed out very long, but Hadleigh had seemed much brighter when they had returned. Magnus had wished them both goodnight and had left them to it. And, observing Hadleigh, she had judged that her emotionally drained brother needed sleep more than he needed her impressing on him the need to return to Pemberton tomorrow.

She would go with him, of course. Her mother could be pretty vicious when she got started; Hadleigh wasn't up to handling that. Taye was not so sure that she could handle it very much better herself.

Perhaps she should arrange to have more than one day away from the office. It was for certain she was not going to leave Pemberton until everything was sorted out in Hadleigh's favour.

She would ring Julian Coombs Comestibles first thing in the morning and—Taye's thoughts broke off mid-thought. The rent on the flat was due this week. She had the cheque already made out and had intended to call in at the agents during her lunch hour the next day to pay. She had already rehearsed what to say to whoever was on the desk: that this was the quarter's rent for Paula Neale at this address. Taye had then planned to make a hasty retreat before anyone could start asking questions.

She could, she supposed, post her cheque with a note to the effect that Paula Neale was away or indisposed and had asked her to send a cheque, but... Taye eventually dropped off to sleep not liking that particular idea very much. It sounded sort of—fishy—somehow. Yet it was important that the rent was paid on time and that everything went smoothly. Various other ideas floated into her head but, probably because by then she was so tired, most of them seemed half baked.

After a few hours' sleep she was up extra early. She slipped on her delicate blue satin kimono over her night-dress and padded quietly to take a look round the sitting room door. Hadleigh was sound away. She left him to his peaceful world and went silently to the kitchen.

She had made a pot of tea and was sitting pensively sipping a cup when a robe-clad Magnus strolled into the kitchen.

'Couldn't sleep?' he enquired.

She could have asked him the same question. He was an habitual early riser, but that morning they were both astir extra early. 'I've a few things to sort out today,' she replied. 'There's tea in the pot.'

Magnus poured himself a cup and brought it over to the table and pulled out a chair. 'You're not going in to work,' he stated, as if it were a fact.

'I'll phone in later and ask for a couple of days off my holiday entitlement,' she replied. And just had to say, 'Thank you for looking after my brother the way you did when he arrived yesterday. He was in a bit of a state, and you were very kind.'

'Kind is my middle name,' he replied, poker-faced, and she had to laugh. He knew as well as she that, up until Hadleigh's arrival, he had been more swinish than kind. 'So what's so heavy that you're going to have to take two days off work to sort it?' he did not refrain from asking.

'Didn't Hadleigh tell you?' she countered.

'I had no need to pry,' Magnus replied. 'But when he started to open up I saw I could either stop him, and let him stew with what was eating him up, or be prepared to listen if he felt so over-burdened that he needed to get it out of his system.'

'How much did he tell you?'

Magnus shrugged. 'Basically that you'd had a raw deal when your mother scuppered your hopes of going to university, and how she has stated she intends to do the same for him. Which seemed to me something of a pity,' Magnus observed, 'because it became clear to me, once we started talking of other things, that Hadleigh is extremely intelligent.'

'He is,' Taye said earnestly. 'Oh, it's not just me that thinks so. You've just said… And, depending on his A level results in August, which are predicted to be close to outstanding, he has been assured of a place at Oxford.'

Magnus was silent for a moment or two. 'But your mother says he is not going?'

'He is going!' Taye replied, the light of battle in her eyes. And found she was explaining, 'Way back, before my father lost his job for speaking up about some bad business accounting he'd come across, we never—um—had to think about money. My mother—' Taye broke off, trying to think up some excuse for the way her mother behaved. 'My mother has always been used to having money. When they split up my father made over his quite considerable fund, inherited from his father, to her, but…' But what? What, kindly, could she say? 'But she's had—um—trouble adjusting—um—financially.'

Magnus, his eyes alert, sharp, took that in, and then enquired, 'What sort of work does your mother do?'

Taye stared at him as if he was mad. Work? Her mother? 'Work?'

'Her career?'

'She—doesn't have one,' Taye replied, having searched for some defence for her mother's preferred idleness without much luck. 'Anyhow, I'll go back with Hadleigh today and see to—er—matters.'

Still looking at Magnus, she thought she saw a warmer kind of light in the grey eyes that regarded her. 'Two days,' he said quietly. 'It's going to take you two days? Sounds as if you're anticipating a few problems?'

Was she ever! 'I might be back tonight.' She tried to inject a lighter note. 'Anyhow, getting my mother to see that Hadleigh must have his chance is only one of my problems.' Taye attempted to get the conversation away from what was very personal to her and her family. But only to find she had slipped up and was then left trying to hold back from revealing something that she had wanted to avoid him knowing anything about.

'What other problems do you have?' he asked, as she—too late—had somehow known that he would.

She wriggled and sought but could not come up with any other problem than the one that was staring her in the face. 'The quarter's rent is due to be paid this week,' she said, meaning to explain that, had she been in London, she would have popped a cheque into the agents in her lunch hour.

Only she did not get the chance. 'You haven't got it!' he accused, that hard-eyed expression she was more familiar with there again. 'You've not only spent the cash I gave you for my share, you've also—'

'*No, I have not!*' she exclaimed hotly, indignantly. Honestly, this man! 'I have a cheque already made out!' she spat furiously. Oh, wouldn't she like to punch his head! 'How *dare* you accuse me of stealing that money you gave me!' She steamed on at top speed, too furiously to be able to sit still—too furiously, as she shot to her feet, to stop and think what she was saying. 'For your information,' she raged—how dared he accuse her of stealing his money?—'I intended to call at Wally, Warner and Quayle in my lunch hour today and hand over the cheque for Paula Neale's rent, and—' She came skidding to a halt, her temper rapidly cooling as, on the instant, she heard what, unthinkingly, she had just said.

Magnus was on his feet too, glaring at her. 'Paula Neale?' He barked the question toughly, as she would have known he would had she paused to think about it. But she had not stopped to think, and now she was sinking into a giant hole of her own making—and she had not the smallest idea of how to get out of it. 'Who the hell is Paula Neale?' he demanded.

'It's nothing to do with you,' Taye answered defiantly.

'Like hell it isn't!' he retorted, an unrelenting look about him that she did not care much for.

'You made me mad!' she said, by way of non-explanation.

'So—give?' he insisted darkly.

'You'll—shop me if I tell you.'

'My patience is wearing thin,' he warned her icily. Oh, go to hell, she fumed! 'Shop you?' Magnus questioned ruthlessly.

Taye sighed. Hadleigh could wake up and come meandering in at any time. She did not want him blundering in to the middle of a storming row. 'Report me,' she explained reluctantly.

'To Wally, Warner and Quayle?' As she had guessed—known—he picked things up quickly. 'Just what have you been up to?' he wanted to know.

Taye had visions of being thrown out of the apartment on her ear—it was all the extra she needed to go with the unpleasant hours she anticipated ahead when she saw her mother. 'Well, if you must know,' she began belligerently—she might be down but she wasn't out—'the tenancy—um—here is not actually in my name.' Oh, my word, his expression had darkened, and it had been pretty dark before. He looked positively barbaric as hands at his sides bunched, almost as if he would physically set about her. 'B-but Paula said, thought, it would be all right to—um—sub-let.'

'Paula?' he barked.

Telling herself that she was not afraid of him, Taye nevertheless did not see any reason to delay answering—she had already told him Paula's name, for goodness' sake.

'Paula Neale,' Taye said quickly, and, not certain that he wouldn't yet set about her if she didn't hurry up with some answers, 'Paula's the actual tenant. I paid my rent to her—she'd already paid it up to this week. Anyhow, the lease is in her name. And—and although I've never actually seen the lease—Paula must have taken it with her when she went.. and—' Taye broke off—Magnus had gone from looking evilly murderous to now looking absolutely dumbstruck. He was still staring at her speechless when Taye feebly tried to regain her thread. 'And—er—Paula got a job out of London and went—'

'Went?' he interrupted tersely.

'Left,' Taye explained, starting to get annoyed again. Confession was supposed to be good for the soul, but she wasn't feeling any better for being made to explain, or by his interruptions. 'She…'

'When did she leave?' he insisted.

Taye threw him an exasperated look. 'About a month before I advertised. I love it here but I realised I couldn't afford to stay here on my own—it's a struggle as it is. But Paula couldn't see any reason not to sub-let. Couldn't have done. I'm her sub-tenant after all.' Taye was starting to feel a shade pink, and did not go a bundle on this confession business. 'Anyhow,' she finished in a rush, 'I sort of got to thinking, Well, I do really love it here, but that perhaps the agents might not be too happy about me sub-letting from Paula and—er—then—um—sub-letting to you, and—'

'My being here being against the terms of the tenancy agreement, you mean?' he butted in, quite mildly, Taye realized, in the face of how chin-thumpingly angry he had seemed before.

'Sort of. Though most of the time I feel sure it is perfectly all right,' she assured him hurriedly. 'It's just that there's this small question mark I have that makes me wonder if the agents will be—well, a bit sticky about it.

If...um—' She broke off as just at that moment her brother wandered in.

But, while she was praying that Magnus would not make a fuss in front of him, he was asking Hadleigh, 'How did you sleep?'

'Like a log,' Hadleigh answered, and, turning to his sister, showing that his sleep had done him quite a lot of good, 'I suppose I'd better go back home.'

'I'll come with you if you like,' Taye said lightly, and caught Magnus looking at her, his expression inscrutable. He knew she was going back with her brother whether Hadleigh wanted her with him or not.

But Hadleigh appeared delighted. 'Will you?' he asked, his face beaming.

'Make yourself a fresh pot of tea while I go and get showered,' she said, filling the kettle and setting it to boil for him as she spoke. She turned to Magnus, 'Er—unless you wanted to shower first?' she asked, grateful that, so far, he wasn't kicking up a fuss.

'After you,' he allowed, though followed her out of the kitchen and caught up with her by her bedroom door. 'If it will make things easier, I can drop your cheque into the agents for you.'

Her beautiful blue eyes widened. 'Would you?' she gasped.

'Quarter's rent for Paula Neale, I think you said.'

'You won't say anything—about...?' she began panickily.

He smiled then, and it was truly a terrific smile, a sincere smile. 'I like living here too,' he replied. Her insides went all funny.

His smile stayed with her while Taye stood under the shower. Had she really...? Had he...? Would he tell...? No. Somehow, she trusted him. She did not know why.

He could be quite, quite awful sometimes. But yet she could not believe that any man with such a sincere genuine smile would turn around and, as it were, stab her in the back.

She and Hadleigh were in Pemberton, going up the drive of her old home, when she began to worry had she been right to trust Magnus Ashthorpe? It was too late then, she knew, to wish she had not told him anything. Though once Paula's name had slipped out he had not given her a chance to do anything other than tell him the rest of it. And, in one way, it was a relief to not have to guard her every word any more.

She had handed over her cheque a few minutes before she and Hadleigh had left. 'You won't...?'

'I won't,' Magnus had replied, had shaken hands with her brother, made some light comment about seeing her when he saw her, and that had been it.

Taye had telephoned her place of employment from the railway station; it had been too early to do so before. She had apologised for the short notice, but explained she had a domestic matter to deal with. 'Anything I can do to help?' her immediate boss had asked, and she had thought how typical that was of the true gentlemen she worked for. They were up to their eyes with work, and yet Victor Richards's first question had been could he help.

'No—no,' she had answered. 'I'll get in as soon as I can.' She did not have to say she would work late to catch up, she was sure he would know that.

She and Hadleigh entered the large imposing residence and one look at her mother's vinegary expression was sufficient to tell Taye that she would be lucky if she cracked her hard exterior in under three days, let alone two.

'Hello, Mother,' Taye greeted her as Hadleigh sloped off to his room.

'How gracious of you to honour us with a visit,' Greta Trafford said by way of welcome.

'You know why I'm here.'

'You could have saved yourself a journey.'

'Hadleigh *is* going to Oxford.'

'And I'm going to the moon. Though first—' as a car was heard pulling up outside '—Larissa and I have a shopping trip arranged. *Do* make yourself at home.' With that, her mother picked up her handbag and went out to greet her friend.

Taye metaphorically dug her heels in. Her mother, despite noticing her overnight bag, would probably not expect her to still be there by the time she got back. Did Taye have news for her!

But it was the following morning before she was able to sit down with her mother and work something out. And by then, if she had not known before, Taye knew why she so loved living in the London apartment. This house, with its elegant fittings, its lush carpets, was a bleak and a cold house, a house without any personal warmth. The night had stretched endlessly; two nights there would be more than was to be endured.

'About Oxford,' she began, breakfast, such as it was, cleared away, her mother's cleaner busy upstairs, and nothing else to occupy her parent just then.

'"That sweet city with her dreaming spires,"' her mother quoted, as if she had no idea to what her daughter was alluding.

'That's the one,' Taye replied, staying calm with difficulty. 'Hadleigh has been assured of a place...'

'Too bad he won't be taking it. Though some other

student whose mother has money to burn will probably be grateful to have his place.'

'You haven't done anything about... You haven't written and said he's not interested?' Taye questioned hotly.

'Not yet,' her mother replied with saccharine sweetness, letting Taye know that it was only a matter of time before she did so.

'He has to go!' Taye stated vehemently.

Greta Trafford shrugged. 'Since you feel so very determined about it, then I suggest you arrange to pay for him.'

'Me?' Taye exclaimed, startled.

'His student loan won't go very far—and he's not getting a penny from me!'

'But...'

'At his age he should be working. Paying for his keep.'

'He works weekends!' Taye protested, knowing without having to ask that their mother would expect him to hand over his earnings, and would not baulk from taking them. 'Hadleigh's bright! He's got a brilliant future in front of him. He...'

Her mother stifled a delicate yawn, and Taye knew then that all the talking in the world was not going to get her mother to change her mind.

But he was going to have his chance. He was. 'I'll pay,' she said firmly. 'Don't do anything—just leave things as they are.'

'*You'll* pay?'

'It was what you suggested.'

'I didn't know you had any money!' Greta Trafford perked up, looking interested for the first time.

Sorry to disappoint. 'I don't have any. I'll have to see about getting a bank loan,' Taye replied. 'Only please don't tell Hadleigh that.'

'You think he's too proud to take your money?'

He must get that from my father, Taye thought acidly, though knew better than to say so. Not that she thought she might bruise her mother's sensitivities—she had few. It was just that Taye did not want to be the cause of her mother being spiteful to Hadleigh over anything she said.

'May I have your promise that, provided it doesn't cost you anything, Hadleigh can go to university?' she asked instead.

Her mother took her time about answering, but eventually agreed. 'I shall be poorer in pocket—you do appreciate that,' she added—and Taye saw in that comment a very big hint that she might be called upon to help out.

Hadleigh went with her to the railway station, which took a two-mile walk, a bus ride for the next four miles, and then another shorter walk. But he was clearly overjoyed. Greta Trafford had magnanimously told him she had reconsidered—and he was bubbling over with relief.

'I don't know what it was you said to Mother, but whatever it was, thanks, Taye.'

'Play as well as work when you get to Oxford,' she replied, having read of students who suffered breakdowns from over-studying.

'I shall do my best.' He grinned, and it was wonderful to her to see his confidence growing by the minute.

It was only when she was in the train on her way back to London that, though fiercely certain that Hadleigh should have his chance, she began to wonder if she had been just a little rash is saying that she would finance him. In terms of money, her outgoings just about kept pace with her incomings. Would the bank play ball?

Surely they would? In almost every post there was some outfit offering to lend money. She would work out her finances and see where she could make savings and then hope her bank manager would feel like being generous.

Meantime she was oh, so glad to be away from that house in Pemberton. The atmosphere there was just so— so unpleasant.

Taye thought of the apartment she shared with Magnus Ashthorpe. Then thought of Magnus himself who, in truth, had been in her mind quite a lot these last two days. She found she was very much looking forward to getting back. Though that was because, after her old home in Pemberton, she loved the flat so well. So well she could not wait to get there. It had nothing to do with the fact that Magnus would be there—of that she was totally certain.

CHAPTER FOUR

THE apartment was empty when Taye got in. She pre-
sumed Magnus was out on some commission. But he
arrived shortly after her and, to make her feel much more
cheerful, seemed to have retained his mild manner. It was
a relief, she owned. She just did not want to have to cope
with his former aggressiveness.

'Everything sorted?' he asked when he saw her, his
eyes searching her face.

She smiled and decided if he could only stay in this
kind of mood she could quite grow to like her flat-mate.
'Yes, thanks,' she replied. 'Busy?' she enquired as he
came to take his ease on the sofa opposite. He was business suited and, she had to admit, looked rather good.

'Doing my bit,' he replied smoothly.

'You've been painting today?' she asked.

'Have to pay my share of the rent,' he answered easily.

But if by mentioning the rent he thought to open up a
discussion about the property they both rented, then Taye
realised she was not yet ready to do so. 'You've never
painted in that suit,' she challenged. The cut of it alone
was just reeking 'expensive', and that was before she
took into account the fine wool material.

'I've been to see a prospective client,' he replied. And,
with a smile that held nothing but charm, 'You thought
artists went around the whole time in paint-stained jeans
and moth-eaten sweaters?'

She could not say she had given the matter very much
thought. 'You leave your—work clothes—at your studio?'

His smile became a grin. 'I didn't think you'd like the smell,' he said—and she just had to laugh.

'Just how successful are you?' she then felt able to ask him.

'I get by,' he replied, and from that she sort of gathered that, for all his expensive suit, he, like herself, sometimes found it a struggle to manage.

She might have said something in empathy with him, only just then the phone rang. She was nearest. She picked it up. It was Julian.

'I stopped by your desk; you weren't there! Mr Richards said you were having a couple of days off?' he queried straight off, and in the sort of tone that suggested he thought she should have acquainted him with such details in advance.

Taye was not so very sure how she felt about his proprietorial attitude and, had Magnus not been there—tuned in to her every word—she might well have made some gentle comment to that effect. But Magnus, showing no sign of intending to leave, *was* there, and she was left explaining, 'I've just got back from paying my mother a visit.'

'Come out with me tonight?' he asked. 'We could…'

She liked Julian, but if he was starting to think that she was his girlfriend on a permanent kind of basis, she wasn't sure that that was what she wanted. 'I've a few things I need to do tonight,' she prevaricated, very conscious of Magnus just sitting there.

'Tomorrow, then?'

She started to feel embarrassed, for herself *and* for Julian. 'I'm free Friday evening if—'

'I'll pick you up. Around seven-thirty?' he promptly accepted.

Taye put down the phone after the call, and owned to feeling a familiar resentment towards her flat-mate. He could have made himself scarce! Had the call been for him, had it been Elspeth, then she would have left him to take his call in private, Taye felt sure.

She looked across at him, but not only was he totally unconcerned that, without saying a word her expression was making her feelings known, he, to her amazement, actually questioned, 'Julian?'

She nodded, and abruptly decided to go and take a shower. During which time she cooled down sufficiently to face that she had grown upset over nothing. Had it been Paula sitting there on the sofa, she would not have expected her to have got up and disappeared.

Feeling a touch shame-faced, she returned to the sitting room. Magnus had his head buried in the newspaper he must have brought in with him. 'I'm sorry I was a bit sniffy earlier,' she said. He slowly lowered his paper and looked at her. She at once felt a fool. 'Shall I make some tea?' she asked quickly.

She saw good humour light his eyes. 'You apologise so beautifully,' he said.

'I've never lived with a man before,' she explained awkwardly. 'Shared a flat-share with a man, I mean. It— it just—it's just a bit of an adjustment to make, that's all.'

'For both of us,' he agreed pleasantly. And suggested, 'Why don't I just sit here and read my paper in the time-honoured way, while you go and bring me a nice cup of tea.'

Doormat? Taye stared at him, in two minds. Then considered how, quite astonishingly, he had made her brother something to eat when he had seen how weighed down and stressed he was, and she reckoned that to make Magnus a drink, and deliver it while he sat there reading his paper, was the least she owed him.

'Anything to eat?' she asked in her best waitress fashion. His mouth picked up at the corners as he shook his head.

Taye went into the kitchen, hardly able to credit that they were getting on so well. When she thought of what a taciturn brute he had been up until Hadleigh had come looking for her, she could hardly credit the change in him.

Perhaps, though, recalling his 'For both of us' just now, he had never lived with a female flat-share before and had initially, as they got used to each other a little, felt a shade awkward about doing so, about making that adjustment too.

She could hardly credit that either. On the face of it he was a sophisticated man. She would have assumed it would take a lot to faze him. It certainly did not bother him to wander around in just his robe. Though, of course, he only wandered from bedroom to bathroom and back again so dressed, and maybe first thing in the morning to the kitchen. But she had witnessed in him an unsuspected sensitivity, so perhaps his adjustment was every bit as great as hers.

Taye took the tray into the sitting room, and as Magnus put down his newspaper and accepted the tea she had poured him she thought that now—now that he knew the facts about the tenancy and wasn't being uptight about it—perhaps they could move forward with much more openness and honesty.

'Er—everything went off all right when you paid the rent in at Wally, Warner and Quayle?' she began, on her new-found spirit of '*glasnost*', a subject which until then she had been at pains to steer clear of.

'I thought you'd never ask,' he replied suavely. Her lips twitched; he hadn't missed her attempts to keep off the subject, then? 'It went without a hitch,' he assured her.

'They didn't notice the signature on the cheque?'

'If they did they probably assumed it was someone paying Miss Neale some funds they owed her.' He paused, then thought to enquire, 'It was *Miss* Neale, I suppose?'

'Oh, yes. Paula isn't married,' Taye replied, and, feeling more comfortable with Magnus, more how their flat-share was meant to be. 'There was someone, but—' She broke off. It was not her business to gossip about her former flat-mate.

'But?' Magnus asked, doing his best too, she realised, to get this flat-mate relationship on a much more friendly basis than it had been.

'Well,' Taye began, 'I don't think Paula would mind me saying that she had been going out with someone for quite a while. And then they started to drift apart.'

'You mean they broke up?' he demanded, rather than asked. But he must have realised he was slipping back into old habits, because he smiled a self-deprecating smile and asked nicely, 'How long ago would that be?'

'It would be around the time Paula asked if I'd like to share. I never ever met Graeme, but Paula used to mention him quite often—and then didn't. And the next thing she had given in her notice at Coombs Comestibles, where we both worked, and had taken a job with some hotel chain on their overseas circuit.' Taye gave him a smile. 'And that's where you came in.'

'And this Graeme—he never came looking for her?'

Magnus asked, surprising her a little because she had thought what she had said had brought them up to date.

'Not so far as I know,' she replied. 'I mean he could have rung Paula on her mobile, for all I know, but I never took a call from him here.'

'Who was he? Any idea?' Magnus asked casually.

Taye shook her head. 'As I said, I've never met him. I've an idea he was something to do with Penhaligon Security—you know, the electronic security equipment people. But that's by the way.'

'So it is,' Magnus agreed. 'I'm here now, not Miss Paula Neale. Do you think she's likely to come back?'

Taye shook her head. 'I'm fairly certain she won't. She said life had got pretty much samey around here and that she wanted to go away and start off fresh somewhere.' Taye smiled as she assured him, 'Your tenancy here is safe, if that's what worries you...' She had never seen anyone looking less worried, but you never knew.

'My sub-tenancy, you mean.'

She felt a touch pink around the gills. 'Er—Mrs Sturgess gave you a terrific reference, by the way,' Taye rapidly took him away from the sub-tenancy subject. He gave the merest inclination of his head. 'But then,' she went on as he took a draught from his teacup, 'she said she had been at school with your mother—' she broke off when he briefly choked on his tea '—so she's probably more like an aunt to you.'

'In the main she has been very kind.' He recovered, and sent Taye a winning smile.

'Her super reference got you half this apartment, at any rate,' Taye replied. And, having opened up with him, felt able to confess, 'Though, to be honest, you were the only applicant. But then the—' She had been about to go on to say that the high rent required must have put other would-be applicants off when something in his expression arrested her. 'What?' she queried, and discovered that he had some confessing of his own to do.

Though he did not seem to look on it as a confession when, entirely untroubled, he openly owned, 'I expect I was the only applicant because I didn't waste any time removing your ad card from the newsagent's window.'

Taye stared at him thunderstruck. 'You did what?' she exclaimed, hardly able to believe her ears. She had waited in that particular weekend! Had watched the road from the dining room window for would-be fellow tenants! Only no other fellow tenant had been around because the flat-share had no longer been advertised! 'When did you?' she gasped.

'When I left here after viewing the apartment,' he answered, completely unabashed.

'Straight away?'

'Within minutes,' he replied, and, that winning smile there again, 'Well, you wouldn't want to share with just any Bill, Jack or Tony, would you?'

'Chance would be a fine thing!' she retorted, still feeling stunned.

'Now you've gone all huffy!' he complained.

In truth she was not feeling all that friendly. She stood up. 'Oh—read your paper!' she instructed snappily. But as she left the room she was certain she heard a smothered laugh coming from behind that raised broadsheet.

In actual fact, when she calmed down a minute or two later and got to thinking about it, she had to laugh too. Though, of course, she would never let him know of it. But she supposed it was funny and, now that it was a *fait accompli,* she rather thought it was better the devil she knew than the one she didn't. And anyhow, if she kicked him out now, what was to stop him from trotting along to Wally, Warner and Quayle and, to coin a phrase, blowing the whistle on her?

Taye wasn't sure she was too happy about having that particular sword dangling over her. But, remembering his kindness to her much troubled brother, she did not truly believe that he would now 'shop' her. Though since, at the moment, they appeared to be ticking over quite nicely, she saw no reason to give him his marching orders. In any event, now that she had paid their quarter's rent, she did not have the means to return to him that which he had paid, so how could she now tell him to go?

She saw little of him for the rest of the week. She stayed late at the office on Thursday and was ready for her bed when she arrived home. She was late on Friday too, and they clashed with bathroom times. 'Provided you're quick, you can have first shower,' he condescended.

For no reason his lofty manner irked her. 'You're out tonight?' she asked snappily. Elspeth? Not that she was that interested anyway, Taye decided sniffily.

'Why should you have all the fun?' he countered, but then asked sharply, 'Are you bringing Coombs back here?'

Taye looked at him, neither liking his question nor his tone. 'Unless you intend to bring your date back!' she retorted. But—and she didn't know what it was about this man, but even in the middle of a spat he could winkle out her sense of humour—'I tell you what, we'll "go to his",' she compromised. Her lips quirked upwards. Her flat-share's did not.

'I've changed my mind—I'll go first,' he grated. And, while she took off at speed, he beat her by a split second and slammed the bathroom door shut between them.

She heard the shower start up, heard him singing—and could have throttled him.

She was right about Julian becoming too proprietorial, Taye discovered later that evening. She could not quite put her finger on what it was: just the warm glance here, or the touch of his hand to her hand, to her arm. She liked him so much and did not want to hurt him. She did not even think that she wanted to stop going out with him—and confessed to being more than a bit mixed up. But as he was driving her home Julian suggested that it was about time that she met his parents ice formed round her feet.

'Some time,' she hedged, having seen his father from a distance at her place of work. She knew she should tell Julian No way, but still did not want to hurt his feelings.

They kissed on parting—he amorously, she starting to panic. She was not sure she enjoyed kissing him any more. Mixed up? Was she ever!

'Shall I see you tomorrow?' he asked as she backed away. 'I can come round early and—'

'I'm doing something with my family tomorrow,' she lied, knowing only that she did not want their relationship to change. Knowing that if it did, she was going to have to stop seeing him. Yet still not wishing to hurt him.

'Sunday's out too, I suppose?'

'I'll see you at the office Monday,' she said brightly, and went indoors feeling fairly flustered. When she walked into the sitting-room it was to see Magnus sitting there nursing what looked like a Scotch. 'You're home early!' she exclaimed in surprise.

'She decided to wash her hair.' Like she would believe that! 'You're looking a little pink-cheeked?' Magnus observed.

She didn't doubt it. 'There's no answer to that,' she replied.

'You've been back to his place,' he accused, his tone suddenly curt.

'No, I haven't!' she denied hotly. 'Not that it's any business of yours anyway.'

'Temper, temper!' he admonished, mocking all at once. But on noticing she looked a little upset, 'What did he do?' he questioned, all mockery gone. But, when she did not reply, 'And do I have to kill him?'

That brought a smile to her lips, but she shook her head. 'He didn't do anything. It's—more me than him.' And, even though it did not seem right to be talking about Julian like this, there was something about Magnus that made her confide, 'I sense—feel—that he, Julian, is getting a bit serious—I'm not sure how to handle it.'

Magnus chewed over what she had said. 'You don't want to marry a rich man?' he teased.

'He didn't ask.'

'You wouldn't consider a poor man?'

'If you're offering—forget it!' Taye retorted, but, as she guessed had been his aim, when he burst out laughing she joined in. 'Goodnight,' she said, and went to bed feeling happier than when she had come in a few minutes earlier.

She decided when she got up on Saturday morning that she would ask Magnus to forget what she had said to him about Julian getting serious. She pattered to the kitchen, knowing she had been wrong to mention it to him—even if it had started to dawn on her that it would be better if she did not go out with Julian again.

Her opportunity to say anything at all to Magnus, however, was scant, when he stepped briefly into the kitchen and, with overnight bag in hand, told her he was off for the weekend.

Something inside of her seemed to plummet, and even as she smiled and wished him, 'Have a good time,' she somehow felt flattened.

That weekend turned out to be one of the longest weekends of her life. The weather had turned sunny, warm and beautiful. But it did nothing to improve her suddenly restless humour. With her chores for the day completed she picked up the book she was currently reading and went and sat outside in the garden. But for once even gazing at the beautiful old apple tree with that twinkling, unshakable and unreachable star stuck in its boughs could not cheer her.

Taye gave up wondering what in thunder was the matter with her. She certainly wasn't the least bit bothered that Magnus Ashthorpe was tom-catting somewhere. She hoped it stayed fine for him—wherever he was!

She tried to get absorbed in her book, but only to have visions of his face float too frequently into her mind. She wondered, sourly, who he was turning on the charm for this weekend—and, impatient with herself, got up and went indoors. She made a snack meal that she was not particularly interested in eating. And, with constant mental interruptions from her absent flat-mate, gave herself up to serious thought on her lack of finances and her promise to financially assist her brother—her mother, actually, because Taye did not want Hadleigh to know about it.

In her view her mother was being most unfair. It was not as if her husband had walked out and left her financially high and dry! She not only had the house, mortgage-free, and all of its paid-for contents, but she also had a substantial monthly sum paid into her bank account as arranged by Alden Trafford. It was not by any means a small amount.

But Taye wondered, not for the first time, would any bank, on the strength of her earnings, allow her to have a loan? And, if they did, bearing in mind her monthly expenditure, how on earth was she going to be able to repay it?

Realising that there was little point in going to the bank until she had figured out how she was going to make repayments on the loan, Taye pulled matters this way and that, and every way she could think of. But, at the end of some very in-depth thinking, she knew that to take on a loan in her present circumstances was just not on. And yet Hadleigh was going to have his chance. About that she was adamant.

Taye considered the possibility of approaching her father, but guessed he lived a pretty much hand-to-mouth existence as it was. He'd had a miserable time of it with her mother but now had the chance of happiness with Hilary. Her father was a proud man and, while he would believe there was sufficient arriving in her mother's bank to fund Hadliegh's years at university, Taye knew in advance he would put Hadleigh in front of his own happiness. He would find the money for his son even if it meant leaving himself penniless and, in his pride, unable to live on his new wife's income. Which in effect he would see as Hilary paying to educate his son. He would, Taye just knew, cancel all idea of marrying Hilary.

Taye considered the possibility of taking an extra job. Perhaps evening and weekend work. Against that, though, she quickly saw, was the fact that she very often worked late in the evening at Julian Coombs Comestibles. And also, if there was some special meeting on, it was not unknown for her to go in on a Saturday too.

All of which meant that if her brother was to have his education—and he was, there was no question about that—then, regrettably, the only answer she could see was that she was going to have to move into somewhere less expensive! With a tremendous bout of reluctance, Taye had to face full on that there just was not anything else that she could do.

The weekend at that point became even more bleak. She did not want to leave. She *loved* it here! She tugged again at her dilemma—but still could not see so much as a glimmer of any other way out.

Taye went to bed that night, her decision made. But, since the rent was paid until the end of September, and Hadleigh would not start at Oxford until the beginning of October, she had close on three months before she would need to take some positive action. Well, say two months, before she gave the agents a month's notice and started looking for—she sighed hopelessly—some relatively inexpensive bed-sit.

Having spent a fractured night plagued with the knowledge that she would have to call and see Wally, Warner and Quayle at some point, Taye left her bed on Sunday morning without enthusiasm. At some point too she was going to have to tell Magnus that by the next quarter day, the twenty-ninth of September, he would have to find somewhere else to live.

When Magnus did not return on Sunday night, Taye went to bed feeling quite disgruntled. By the look of it, he wouldn't care anyway that she was giving up the apartment. All too clearly he had no trouble finding somewhere else to rest his head!

Julian came to see her at her desk on Monday. 'Fancy having a bite somewhere tonight?' he asked. 'I'm off to our Edinburgh office tomorrow for a couple of days.'

'Umm... Do you mind if we leave it a while?' she replied, and felt upset that he looked upset.

'Fine,' he said quietly and, having quite a busy job himself, went back to his own office.

Taye had a feeling that she had not handled that very well, and was in the middle of wondering how better she could have handled it when she received a call from a man she knew vaguely from a party she and Julian had been to not so long ago.

'Damien Fraser,' he introduced himself. 'We met at Sandy Stevenson's party. I expect you've forgotten me, but...'

'Of course I remember you, Damien,' she answered pleasantly. Tall, blond, affluent and, if she remembered rightly, going around with a very attractive brunette. 'What can I do for you?'

'Have dinner with me?'

'Have...' Her mouth fell open; she hadn't been expecting that.

'You and Julian Coombs aren't an item?' he asked. 'I'm not stepping on his toes?'

'Er...' she hedged. They were not an item, and she knew now indelibly, without actually knowing how she knew, that they were never going to be an item. 'Er—no,' she said. 'But aren't you going steady with...?'

'She dumped me,' he said, sounding so remarkably cheerful about it that either, as she suspected, he had done the dumping or he was not particularly bothered.

Taye decided that she quite liked him. Especially since he was allowing his ex-girlfriend her pride by letting it be known that she had dumped him. But Taye was not sure that she wanted to go out with him just the same. He was somehow just a touch brash for her tastes. And anyhow, she had not yet broken with Julian.

'Dinner?' Damien urged.

'I'm not sure of my immediate plans,' she demurred. 'If you'd like to give me your phone number, I'll get back to you.'

Without a moment's hesitation he gave her his home and business phone numbers, included his mobile phone number, added, 'Don't keep me waiting too long, Taye,' and then said goodbye.

Taye supposed it was quite pleasant to know that someone wanted to take her out. But when she went home that night she had no idea when, or even if, she would ever ring any of the numbers Damien Fraser had given her.

She let herself into the apartment, musing she would make herself a tasty Spanish omelette and... She discovered that Magnus was not home. All at once she did not feel very hungry.

Her heart oddly lifted when around eight o'clock she heard his key in the lock. Good grief, as if she cared if he never came home! 'The wanderer returns!' she commented when, tall, all male and good-looking with it, he strolled in, weekend bag in hand.

He stopped in his tracks—she supposed she had sounded far more acid than she had meant to. 'What did I do?' he asked.

She knew she had earned that, but affected to be off-hand. 'You tell me.' Quickly she countermanded that. 'No, don't. What you get up to when you're away from here is absolutely nothing to do with me.'

'You're right,' he retorted crisply. 'It isn't.' He paused then, though, and, his glance suddenly speculative, 'Though for a moment there I got the impression you were a wee bit—jealous.'

Taye stared at him in astonishment. 'Oh, please!' she exclaimed in disgust, and picked up her book that was never going to get read at this rate. He went to his room and she read the same line ten times as she fumed at the ridiculous notion that she was in any way jealous.

She tried to read, heard the shower running, and decided to make a warm drink and take it, and herself, off to bed. She was still in the kitchen when a robe-clad Magnus Ashthorpe appeared and decided to make toast. What he put on his toast was up to him, but, not wanting to go to bed as if they were no longer on speaking terms, 'Don't forget to wipe up your toast crumbs,' she offered, quite pleasantly.

'What?'

As if he did not know what she was talking about! 'You have a habit of leaving breadcrumbs littered about,' she reminded him evenly.

'I do?'

'I was—suggesting—you clean up after yourself.'

'Well, that's a new experience!'

She wasn't with him. 'What is?'

'Being bossed about by a woman.'

'I wasn't bossing!' she informed him heatedly. 'I was merely…' She felt exasperated suddenly. 'If you want to encourage mice that's up to you!' she told him shortly.

He smiled. He looked at her and actually smiled as, silkily, he replied, 'I'm so glad I came back.'

Taye went to bed without her warm drink. She huffed out of the kitchen, leaving her beaker on the countertop—she would rather die of thirst than go back for it. And he, the sarcastic brute, did not bother to knock on her door to either tell her about it or bring it in.

Taye was still smarting over his 'jealous' remark when

she was sitting at her desk the next morning. As if! Ridiculous. Totally ridiculous! But, no matter how she dismissed the notion, it still niggled away at her.

Which was perhaps why, when in the late afternoon Damien Fraser again rang, and suggested she may have lost his phone numbers, and when he again asked her out, she said yes. And, what was more, she gave him her address so he should call for her that night.

She was not sure, five minutes after putting down the phone, that it was such a bright thing to have done. But by then it was too late. She had still not done anything about Julian, and it normally just was not her way to date one man while going out with another.

Taye was in her room getting ready to go out with Damien that night when she paused to consider that nothing seemed normal any more. She was in the middle of wondering when the start of 'not normal' had begun— was it before Hadleigh's crestfallen visit, or before…?— when she thought she heard the sound of the door buzzer.

She glanced at her watch. If that was Damien, he was around fifteen minutes ahead of time! She was almost ready. She applied a finishing touch of lipstick, drew a comb through her hair and made it to the sitting room in time to see Magnus bringing Damien in.

'I'm early,' Damien apologised, looking at her as if he thought she was as good to look at as he remembered. 'I wasn't sure I knew the way here—I didn't want to be late.'

She smiled. There was not much else she could do. But at least Magnus Ashthorpe could put that in his 'jealous' hat and eat it. Did she look jealous? Huh! Damien was somewhere in his late twenties, he dressed well and, she supposed some would say, was quite a catch. Good for the non-jealous ego, if nothing else.

She set about introducing the two. 'Damien—my flat-share, Magnus Ashthorpe—Damien Fraser,' she completed. Though it appeared they had already done the honours themselves.

'I was just saying to Magnus that I seem to know his face from somewhere,' Damien commented.

'Magnus is an artist,' Taye supplied.

'Perhaps we've met at some function or other,' Damien remarked.

'Perhaps,' Magnus agreed, but Taye got an impression that he thought it unlikely.

'I own Fraser Future Investments.' Damien seemed to think he should say what work he did. 'We're doing extremely well,' he announced without modesty.

'I'm sure,' Magnus murmured urbanely.

'Shall we go?' Taye jumped in, sending a smile to her escort.

At the start of the evening she had quite a pleasant time. But as the evening wore on Taye formed the view, from his comments and the unexpected leading remark Damien made, that he was more forward than Julian. But she smiled and chatted while being unable to refrain from comparing that while Julian was probably in the same financial bracket he was much less boastful about it.

Strangely Magnus kept popping into her head, and she could not help but think that while he was nowhere near as affluent—by comparison probably on his uppers—there was still something genteel about him. Sophisticated, yes; genteel, yes; sensitive... Good grief! Forget the wretched man.

'Let's go on to a nightclub?' Damien suggested with a wide smile that held none of the charm of her flat-share's. 'I know a super club,' Damien enthused. And, with a not so surreptitious lingering glance to her bosom, 'Or if you'd rather we could go back to my place, listen to some music and—'

'Actually,' Taye cut in, feeling decidedly uncomfortable, 'tomorrow's a work day.' Thank goodness. 'I think I'd better go home, if you wouldn't mind.' She knew that home was where she was headed whether he minded or whether he didn't.

'Oh, no!' he exclaimed, giving her the full horrified treatment.

'Oh, yes! I have a busy day tomorrow,' Taye stated pleasantly, but firmly, adding a smile.

He took the hint. 'Perhaps we can do this again on Friday?' he suggested. 'No work Saturday.'

Perhaps we can't! She had dipped her toe in a different pond. It felt alien. She knew it would not get any better. Whether he took her silence for agreement she did not know, but he drove her home without further objection.

Though did think to ask, as he drew up at her door, 'Will your flat-mate still be up?'

She would get him out of bed if he wasn't. 'He's usually working on something in the sitting room long after I've gone to bed,' she invented, having no idea what Magnus did once she had closed her bedroom door. But there was no way she was going to offer Damien the coffee he was all too obviously angling for. 'Thank you for a lovely evening,' she trotted out as a prelude to making her escape.

'Friday?' he asked.

'I'm sorry. I've a family thing on this weekend,' she excused, hoping he and Julian would never get around to comparing notes.

'How about—?'

'I really must go.' She cut him off, reaching for the car door handle.

Only as she reached for the door Damien reached for her and pulled her back. 'Don't I get a little reward?' he asked, in what she assumed he thought was his sexy voice. And before she could tell him not a chance, he had grabbed her in a suffocating hold.

She gave him an almighty shove for his trouble, and was fortunately able to evade his mouth, his kiss landing somewhere to the side of her head. '*Don't!*' she yelled angrily, bunching her hands and giving him another hefty shove. She did not want to be kissed by him, or by Julian, or by anybody else for that matter. Weirdly—even as she was pushing Damien forcefully away—she thought of Magnus.

Weird was not the word for it, in her opinion, though in times of stress who could account for what went through one's mind?

'I read it wrong, didn't I?' Damien said by way of apology as he let go his hold.

You can say that again! She followed through her earlier intention of getting out of the car. 'Goodnight,' she managed civilly, and left him sitting there. She had closed the outer door of her building behind her before she heard him start his car engine.

She owned to be feeling upset, which, under the circumstances, she considered was not surprising. She recalled his brute force and shuddered at how she would have fared had she been daft enough to go back to his place. No wonder she had thought of Magnus earlier. He had been yards away. Perhaps if she'd had to scream, and had screamed loud enough, he would have come to her aid.

Having been able to analyse why Magnus had sprung

to her mind when she was realising that she did not want Damien's kisses, or Julian's either, Taye let herself into the apartment.

She still felt a little shaken from the way Damien Fraser had grabbed her. What she just did not need as she walked into the sitting room was to have Magnus Ashthorpe blast at her, 'Playing the field?'

She knew what he meant. Julian one night, Damien another. But she was rattled. 'I'm not giving myself to just any man, that's for sure!' she snapped.

'Huh! Saving yourself for your future husband?' Magnus jibed scornfully—and her already out of sorts disposition fractured completely and her temper went rocketing.

'It's what we virgins do!' she hurled at him, and sorely wanted to hit him.

His look was totally sceptical. 'At least that's what you're going to claim when you sell yourself to—'

'Don't be disgusting!' she erupted hotly. But, having cut him off, she knew she was losing it. Her voice was all shaky and she was close to tears. She swallowed hard. Opened her mouth to give him an earful—only then something in her seemed to crumble. Taye made a dive for her bedroom.

Had she hoped, however, to have some space, some time alone in which to get herself back together, then she soon discovered that she did not stand a chance. Because Magnus, with barely little pause, must have taken off after her. He was in her bedroom with her at any rate before she had time to close the door.

'Clear off!' she yelled, still swallowing hard.

'Aw, don't cry. Please, Taye, don't cry,' he urged, and came to her and made to take her into his arms.

'Don't you come near me!' she hissed fiercely, tears

glinting on her lashes. 'I thought you were genteel, sensitive—but you're a—a pig!'

'It's true,' he agreed. 'And you hate me.'

'And I...' He had done it again! He had made her laugh! There was no sense to it. She did hate him. At that very moment she hated him like fury—but he still had the power to make her laugh at the most unexpected of moments. She turned her back on him. 'I'm all right now,' she mumbled, letting him know that she was not going to break down in floods of tears so he could go away.

She heard him move; but not away from her. He came closer, and turned her to face him. 'What brought this on?' he asked gently, one hand coming beneath her chin to tilt her head up so he should see into her eyes.

'You don't think you had anything to do with it?'

Magnus smiled that smile she had once seen as sincere, that smile that would charm the birds from the trees. 'I'm a pig; we've established that,' he agreed. 'But I think, on reflection, you were upset about something when you came in.' A sudden glint came to his eyes. 'What did Fraser do?' he questioned toughly.

She did not want to tell him but, tenderly almost, Magnus all at once gathered her into his arms. And suddenly, as he held her gently cradled in his arms—arms that somehow seemed to be far more comfortable than any other man's hold—she found she was telling him, 'Damien didn't do anything so very bad. And I suppose it must be more me than him—my discovering that I didn't like him as much as I thought I did.'

'He's not going in your little black book, then?' Magnus coaxed.

'Poor man,' she said, feeling a bit shame-faced now she thought about it. 'Though when he made one or two leading comments I should have seen that he'd expect a kiss goodnight.'

'Did he get one?' Magnus asked, his arms tightening a little as he held her.

Taye shook her head. 'I think I might have thumped him. I can't be sure.'

'That should have cooled his ardour.'

'He let me go, anyway,' she agreed. 'But I was still upset when I came in—only to have you accuse me of selling myself to the highest bidder!' He had not actually said that, but she was sure he would have done had she not cut him off.

'Pig's too fine a name for me,' he said nicely.

'Oh, you...' she mumbled, and was astonished at the thrill that shot through her, and how good it felt when Magnus gently dropped a kiss on the tip of her dainty nose.

He was still gently cradling her when he asked, 'Do I take it you won't be seeing Fraser of Fraser Future Investments again?'

She had to smile. She had dashed to her room feeling anything but like smiling, but here she was... 'True,' she answered, sobering. 'That's one more off my list.'

'List?'

'The list of wealthy eligibles you seem certain I have.'

'You'll probably end up marrying some poor man and having half a dozen babies who will keep you poor—' Magnus broke off as she shook her head.

'I'd rather stay single than marry a poor man,' she told him seriously.

'That bad?' he enquired.

And all at once, and slightly to her own amazement, she found she was confiding, 'My father came from mon-ied people and earned a top salary. But it—the money—

all sort of disappeared around the time he lost his job. But even before that I grew up in a household where any love my parents had for each other was soured over money. When the money started to run out—it became intolerable.' Taye shuddered in his hold. 'The rows were constant—that's not going to happen to me.'

'You think it might?' he asked seriously.

She gave a shrug of her shoulders. 'Apparently, while I feature my mother physically, according to her I'm my father through and through. But that still makes me my parents' daughter—I'm not risking it.'

'They've damaged you, haven't they?' he said softly. 'Between them they—'

'I don't know about that,' Taye cut in quickly.

'You don't think, aware of all the pitfalls, that you won't take extra care to not end up being the same?'

'I'll take jolly good care; that's a given,' she answered. 'I still won't be risking that pauper—and the parcel of offspring you seem to think goes with it.'

'You're forgetting one thing, though,' he said.

'And that is?' She did not think she had forgotten anything. The idea of ending up like her parents had been— the endless bickering, the daily explosions into furious rows, her mother's voice raised to near screaming pitch, the rows, oh, the endless rows, before her father had left home—that sort of life was just not to be considered.

'You have forgotten, little Taye, that you are a person in your own right. You are not your mother who, when I look at you, must be beautiful on the outside, and nor are you your father who, when I talk to you, I know must have an inner goodness.'

'You think I have an inner goodness?'

'You have an outer beauty that is matched by your inner self,' Magnus assured her warmly.

'Oh, Magnus,' she whispered, and felt near to tears again. 'I think that's the nicest thing anyone has ever said to me.'

She was still feeling much moved by what he had said when his head came down and very gently he slowly, unhurriedly, laid his lips over hers.

And when he eventually pulled back, Taye felt utterly incapable of speech.

Which made it just as well that Magnus had no such problem. 'Go to bed, sweetheart,' he told her. 'But remember and keep it in mind that whatever has happened in your past you must not let it cloud your future. You are your own person—and a very nice person at that.'

Taye was still standing there spellbound when, his arms falling away from her, Magnus stepped back, seemed to look at her as if to check she would be all right, and then left her.

Left her staring after him. She remembered his kiss, long and lingering—and unthreatening. He had kissed her, and she had not objected. How could she? His kiss was the most wonderful kiss she had ever known.

He had held her in his arms, and she had never imagined such an incredibly comfortable hold. He thought her beautiful too, inside and out.

Without question he must obviously be seeing her with his artist's eyes. But his kiss, his hold, his sensitivity... Taye went to bed knowing that she would not sleep. But, strangely, she did. Somehow she felt at peace within herself—and with him.

CHAPTER FIVE

TAYE was not at peace with herself the following day. While it was a fact she did wake up with a smile on her face, once she began analysing the happenings of the previous evening, after her date with Damien Fraser, she began to feel more than a touch edgy.

She thought about Magnus's kiss, his wonderful kiss, and any peace she had known was, in the light of morning, shattered. They were flat-mates, she and Magnus, and that was all that they were. They were not kissing flat-mates, nor did she want them to be.

She got out of bed, but did not go straight to take her shower. But stood at her door for several hesitating seconds. Then she heard the distinctive sound of the door into the main hall closing and locking. Magnus was up bright and early, and away about his business.

Still Taye did not move, but remembered again his kiss, how comfortable his arms. For all his kiss had lingered, it had been unhurried and she had at no time felt threatened. It had been a giving kiss, not a taking kiss. He'd asked for nothing but to comfort her and she...

Taye was at her office before it came to her that she had been pretty much mesmerised by the feel of Magnus Ashthorpe's well-shaped mouth over hers. Had she not been so mesmerised, who knew? She might well have responded!

Shaken by that realisation, she was horror-struck when she thought of what Magnus's reaction would have been had she held on to him and kissed him back. She felt hot

91

all over just thinking of what *his* realisation would have been that she misread what his unthreatening kiss meant. Which she now saw had only been to take away the unpleasant experience she'd had with Damien Fraser.

Such thoughts haunted her through most of that day. As a consequence she felt awkward about going back to the apartment she shared with him.

In no hurry to go home, she decided to put in an extra hour or two at her desk. Which made it nearer eight than seven when she got in. But only to discover she need not have bothered trying to keep out of his way. Magnus did not come home at all that night. And that—peeved her.

So much so that when she bumped into him in the kitchen the next evening, she had moved from any feeling of awkwardness to a feeling of hostility with him.

'Hello,' she managed.

'Good day?' he enquired coolly.

'Fair,' she replied.

It was about the sum total of their conversation that night. She did not feel much like talking to him—he, likewise, clearly could not be bothered.

Treating the place like some hotel, she fumed when she went, early, to bed. It wouldn't take much for her to tell him in the morning that come the end of September he would have to find some other 'hotel' to rent.

By Friday Taye was starting to feel a wee bit ashamed of herself. What was the matter with her, for goodness' sake? She had been behaving downright cranky. While it was true Magnus had not exactly been doing cartwheels of joy across the kitchen floor last night, he had every right to treat the place as a hotel if he wanted to. He had scraped together the rent, which made it now his home. Home was his base, and with the likes of Elspeth, not to mention Pen—or Penny—Penelope—around, well, for heaven's sake, you only had to take in the virile look of the man to know that there would be occasions when he might find the call of a different place to rest his head of more interest.

Taye frowned, felt something akin to sickness in the pit of her stomach, and realised she needed something to eat. Before she could leave her desk, though, a colleague she was friendly with rang through on the internal phone to invite her to an impromptu kind of party she had just decided to throw on the following evening.

'You've probably got a date, so no need to say yes or no now. But if he's really dishy, bring him too.'

Taye had to smile. But no sooner had she cleared that call than a call came through on an external line. It was Damien Fraser. 'How do you feel about a nightclub tonight?' he asked warmly.

I'd rather glue my feet to the floor! 'I'm—er—seeing someone tonight,' she replied, and could not help wondering why she was trying to spare his feelings.

Silence for a moment. 'How about Saturday?'

You would have thought he'd give up! 'I'm sorry Damien, I—um—it doesn't feel right to me to go out with you when I'm seeing someone else.'

'I don't mind,' he declared at once. She couldn't think of a reply to that, but guessed he must have cottoned on. 'You still have my phone numbers?'

She was glad to have said goodbye to him, but only to realise that as if by auto-suggestion—call it what you will—in telling him she was seeing someone else that night she had conjured up Julian.

It was Julian's first day back since his Edinburgh trip, and she had hoped that when she had asked him to 'leave it a while' he might leave it longer than this. 'I wonder how you feel about having a break from London this weekend?' he asked. 'We could go tonight after work. There's an MG rally in—'

'Oh, I don't think so, Julian,' she cut in quickly, gently.

'You could have your own room,' he urged, and, to make her smile, 'If you absolutely insist.'

'You're a gem, Julian. But do you mind if I say no?'

'Yes, I mind,' he replied, but smiled too, and bent and dropped a kiss on her cheek. 'Would *you* mind if I went without you?'

Taye went home that night knowing for certain that, much though she did not want to hurt Julian, she was going to have to tell him that she would not go out with him again. The very fact that he had asked if she would mind if he went to the rally alone, as if they were joined at the hip or something, told her she had better tell him before too long. She did not look forward to doing it.

Neither did she look forward to going back to the apartment after work. If Magnus was in the same taciturn frame of mind tonight, they were in for a very jolly weekend! That was, should her flat-mate deign to delight the apartment with his presence that weekend. For all she knew he would be taking his weekend bag and 'delighting' some other abode—some other female—with his company.

At that point Taye brought herself up short. She had already run the gamut of his 'treating the place like some hotel'. It was where he lived, for goodness' sake. He was perfectly entitled to tote his weekend bag wherever he wished. And, not forgetting by any means that he had not come home on Wednesday night, perfectly entitled to take his overnight bag with him in the week too if he wanted to.

They were busy at the office which meant she was late

leaving. But Taye eventually went home, having deter-mined that since she and Magnus were stuck with each other she must make more of an effort.

To that end, she breezed into the apartment, into the sitting room, and, Magnus home first, smiled when she saw him, long legs stretched out in front of him, reading his paper.

''Lo, Magnus,' she greeted him brightly, and, heading for the kitchen, 'Fancy a cup of tea?'

Silence. She kept on walking. 'I'll join you in a pot,' he finally accepted as she reached the kitchen door.

She felt cheered, happy suddenly. She put her bag down, set the kettle to boil, washed her hands at the kitchen sink and proceeded to load a tray. Once the tea was made she carried the tray into the sitting room.

'Read your paper,' she instructed when he lowered it. 'You don't have to—'

'And if I want to?'

She hid a smile. 'Are you out tonight?' she asked, handing him a cup of tea.

He put his paper to one side. 'I thought I'd stay home,' he answered.

'Obviously saving your strength!' was out before she could stop it. Magnus looked at her, one eyebrow slightly aloft, causing her to feel slightly pink. 'Sorry.' She apol-ogised for her remark.

His expression stayed pleasant; she took it as a sign she was forgiven. 'You?' he asked. 'Are you home—or out on the tiles?'

Her on the tiles! He could talk! 'I had a couple of offers,' she confessed, not to let the side down. 'You know how it is.'

He nodded, but, after the grumpy brute he had been the night before, was charm personified when he replied,

'I'm surprised there were only two. Which one did you accept?'

'Neither.'

'Ah!' Magnus murmured. 'Fraser Future Investments blotted his copybook on Tuesday and you've decided not to give him a second chance. But—Julian Coombs?' he left it there, though after a moment queried, 'Backing off, Taye?'

She bit her bottom lip worriedly. 'I don't want to hurt him.'

For a second she thought she espied a kind of warmth in the grey eyes that studied her. But his expression was steady as he advised, 'Then end it. End it sooner rather than later.'

She had already decided to do so, but thought to change the subject. 'That's enough about my love-life. Or lack of it,' she added with a light laugh. And was about to go on to ask about his work, a subject that strangely had never come up, when Magnus spoke first.

'Is it true?' he asked.

'Is what true?' she replied, mystified.

'Your—lack of love-life.'

She stared at him. 'My lack...' Suddenly it clicked what he was referring to. 'I've—had my moments,' she said defensively—and saw him smile.

'But,' he went on, determined, it seemed, to be answered, 'you've never actually—tiptoed through the tulips?'

The cheek of the man! Though, since it was she who had brought up the fact that she was a virgin in the first place, perhaps he, this time, could be forgiven. 'No, I haven't,' she admitted. 'And, no,' she hurried on, 'before you ask, I don't have a hang-up about—about such matters.'

Magnus looked into her lovely blue eyes, his expression softening. 'You're sure?' he asked. 'Most girls start experimenting early…'

'I'm not most girls,' she cut him off.

'I think I'm beginning to discover that,' he remarked quietly.

'And I don't think I feel very comfortable with this conversation.'

'There—and I thought we could tell each other everything,' he mocked.

She wanted to laugh, but wouldn't. Sometimes she didn't know whether to hit him or kiss him. Kiss him? Weird—where had that notion strayed in from? 'I've never seen any of your work,' she said abruptly.

'How about that for a quick change of topic?' he commented, and she had the weirdest notion that he was trying to avoid discussing his work. Weird—it was her day for weird!

'Have you any of your paintings here?' she pressed.

'You wouldn't want them cluttering up the place.'

'I suppose it takes ages for the paint to dry,' she lobbed back. He wasn't the only one who could be determined to stick with the subject.

'Depends which medium you use,' he informed her.

'Which one do you use?' He gave her a look she read as saying For goodness sake shut up. 'Indulge me?' she requested lightly.

'Oils, mainly,' he decided to yield.

'What subject matter?'

'You really do have the bit between your teeth!'

'Landscapes?' she suggested.

'Portraits,' he answered, and, should she be feeling smug, he changed the topic this time—to talk of something she had absolutely no wish to talk about. 'I didn't mean to kiss you the other night,' he said, quite out of the blue.

It could have been, she reflected, that Magnus had been feeling awkward too ever since that kiss, but she doubted it had preyed on his mind as much as it had on hers. 'Pfff—I never gave it another thought,' she answered off-handedly, on the basis that if you are going to tell a lie, make it a whopper! 'I was going to make myself a snack. Have you eaten?' she asked, getting to her feet and re-loading the tray.

Taye took herself off to bed early that night. Magnus had already eaten and required nothing, and, truth be told, she never knew what subject of conversation he would start on next. Perhaps it was because, prior to sharing with him, she had never gone in for such open sort of conversations but, recalling the personal matters that had come up for discussion, she felt that enough was enough for one night.

Which in her view made it peculiar that, when Saturday mornings were usually a chance for her to have a lie-in, she should feel the urge to get up and get to the kitchen, lest Magnus decided to go off early somewhere, as was not unknown.

She decided tea first, then shower, and padded off to the kitchen and had the kettle boiling when, showered and dressed, Magnus strolled in, his eyes on her white-blonde hair.

'You look very fetching with your hair all messed up like that,' he commented, his eyes on her all-over-the-place hair. She felt a little pink, very self-conscious, and pushed straightening fingers through her hair, then tight-ened her satin kimono at the waist. 'Sorry,' he apologi-sed, observing her blush. 'I didn't mean to embar-rass you.'

'This—um—flat-share business takes a bit of getting used to,' she mumbled, and turned from him to pour boiling water into the teapot.

'It doesn't worry you, though?' he asked. She set the kettle down, and, turning to face him, had never seen him more serious.

'Given that you're a surly brute sometimes—though I'll admit not so bad now as when you first came here— I'm not at all worried.'

His glance remained steady on her, as if he was satisfying himself that she was speaking the truth. Then, 'Good,' he said, and asked, 'What are your plans for today?'

For one heart-sprinting moment she thought he was asking her out. Common sense nailed that one on the head. He was a worldly-wise man; his tastes would lie with worldly-wise women. 'Oh, there's a party I'll probably go to tonight—one of my colleagues from work,' she explained. 'Apart from that, there's washing, ironing, some shopping, some cleaning thrown in,' she answered lightly. 'A bit of this, a bit of that. You?' she asked.

'Mainly that,' he replied, which told her precisely nothing.

'You could help with the cleaning if you like?' she said generously.

'I don't suppose it's every day you get such an offer turned down, but I'll give that one a miss, if you don't mind.'

She had to smile. 'I didn't really think you'd agree— I just wanted to see the whites of your eyes.'

Magnus gave her a playful tap on the nose, took a step closer, and she had the strangest notion that he was about to embrace her. But instead he took a hasty look at the kitchen clock and, remarking, 'I'm going to be late!' did not stop for a cup of tea, but went.

No sooner had the outer hall door closed than Taye was hurrying to the dining room. It was from her vantage point by the window that she saw him swing out of the building and, overnight bag in hand, go striding down the street.

Disappointment hit her like some dark cloud. Even while she was telling herself that she did not care one iota that he would not be coming home tonight, and probably not tomorrow night either, she could not deny feeling quite ridiculously down about it.

And it was ridiculous. She should not give a button, but she did. She recalled how her heart had hurried up its beat when she had thought him on the point of asking her out. And Taye faced then that, having started off quite disliking the man, she now not only liked him but was quite attracted to him.

And that would never do! They were flat-mates, and that was all. Flat-mates who happened to be of the opposite sex. Attraction just did not come into it. So Taye told herself as she cleaned, dusted and attended to laundry.

Perhaps it was just as well that, come late September, they would go their separate ways. She had been on the point of telling him that morning that she would be giving up the tenancy; not that it was hers to give up, in actual fact. There had been an excellent opening when they had been discussing their mixed flat-share, but either the moment had got away from her—or she had been reluctant to end their joint tenancy.

Reluctant to end their tenancy! Taye backtracked on that thought. Well, it was not that she was reluctant to end *their* joint tenancy, dope. It was just that going back to live in a bed-sit had no appeal whatsoever. That was the only thing she was reluctant about.

Taye managed to keep herself fully occupied during the day. After completing her domestic chores she went shopping for a few groceries, checking the post on the main hall table on her way out. Nothing for her—and who was Mr M. A. Penhaligon? she wondered of the parchment envelope reposing there. She did not think there was a new tenant; perhaps Rex Bagnall or the Davieses had someone staying?

Penhaligon was not a name she came across very often. In fact she had only come across it before in connection with Penhaligon Security, where she thought Paula's ex worked. She opened the main door into the street and as thoughts of Magnus started to intrude so the name Penhaligon went from her mind.

By early evening, her weekend chores completed, Taye began to feel restless. Somehow she just could not seem to settle. She decided to give Hadleigh a call. She might just catch him before he pedalled off to his restaurant job. She worried about him pedalling the five miles home in the dark late at night, but her mother had pursuits other than those of going to pick up her son, so bicycle power it had to be.

'Hello, Mother,' Taye greeted her pleasantly. 'Um—everything all right?'

'And if it's not?'

And if it's not what are you going to do about it? was what her mother meant. 'Going somewhere nice?' Taye asked, keeping her tone pleasant. There was no question of her mother staying home on a Saturday night.

'Larissa is having a dinner party. I'm in the middle of getting ready.'

In other words, state your business and hang up. 'Is Hadleigh there?'

'Oh, he went ages ago!'

'He's already left?'

'He's working extra hours today.'

There seemed little more to say. Soon her mother would grow impatient and would bluntly ask her why she had called. Taye inwardly sighed; she had given up wanting a warmer relationship with her parent. You could only bang your head against a brick wall for so long.

'I'll see you soon,' she said.

'I'll look forward to it.' They didn't come any more insincere than her mother!

Feeling more down than ever suddenly, Taye did not feel very good company just then, and decided against going to the party.

Around eight she took herself off to indulge in a long hot soak in the bath. To lie there getting prune-fingered was a luxury. Conscious as she was not to hog the bathroom, it was usually a quick shower and out. But tonight she had the apartment to herself; she just did not want to think about Magnus and where he might be.

Which was obviously at some female's house or apartment; he would not be able to afford to live it up at some fancy hotel somewhere. All Taye sniffily hoped was that Elspeth, or whoever, was the domesticated sort who believed in fifty-fifty and made him vacuum the place through tomorrow before he left. Or, before whenever he left. It had been a Monday night before he had come home once, she easily recalled.

But she was not going to think about him. Deliberately, and not for the first time, she turned her thoughts away from the man she shared the apartment with. The bathwater was going cold. Should she heat it up or get out?

Such major decisions were suddenly and abruptly swiped from her mind when she thought she heard the sound of a door closing. She began to pull herself up, her head cocked to one side listening, when, to render her horrified—not to say bereft of speech—the bathroom door opened and Magnus came in!

For stunned moments—it could have been seconds—they stared at each other, Magnus equally dumbstruck as his glance took in her white-blonde hair, pinned all any old how to the top of her head, her naked and wet shiny body, and her beautifully rounded breasts with their hardened pink tips now that she had chilled a little. Taye was still half lying there as his gaze travelled down her body.

Then with a flurry of arms she struggled to sit up and double over to hide herself from his view. 'I didn't—' she managed hoarsely.

'I thought—' he began.

And at the sound of his voice Taye suddenly came to life. '*Get out!*' she screeched, and was glad he did not stay to argue but, turning smartly about, was already on his way.

Shaken and distressed, Taye felt in one giant turmoil. Oh, how dreadful! She suddenly saw herself as he must have seen her—naked, her breasts on view, her belly, her... In a flurry, as though hoping to escape the picture she must have made, Taye quickly got out of the bath.

She felt aflame from top to toe, and did not know how she was ever going to face him. Hastily she towelled herself dry, then wondered just why she was hurrying. She was in no rush to see him again.

Donning the fresh nightdress she had brought in with her, but still feeling too hot all over to bother with her kimono, Taye cleaned the bath and tidied up after her. Then, knowing she could delay no longer, but hoping to avoid seeing Magnus, she shrugged into her kimono, opened the bathroom door—and bolted to her bedroom.

Though any feeling of relief she might have experienced to have made it that far without seeing him was short lived, when all at once there came a light tapping on her door! It was on the tip of her tongue to yell at him to go away. But her feelings of being upset were all at once mingling with a most peculiar but not to be denied urge to see him.

Despite that, she was still not feeling very friendly towards him when she went to the door and yanked it open. 'Yes?' she demanded.

Magnus eyed her, his grey eyes steady on her crimson face. 'Did anyone ever tell you you have truly a most beautiful body?' he had the utter nerve to pleasantly enquire.

Her mouth fell open from the sheer audacity of the man. On the instant her embarrassed colour faded. 'I was expecting a profuse apology at the very least!' she exploded. But, as she stood glaring hostilely at him, Taye suddenly caught a gleam of devilment in his eyes, and she knew she was not going to like what he said next, and that was before he said it.

'I should like to say that I'm very sorry that I'm— um—the only one to have ever seen you—er—knicker- less,' he began, 'but I'm not.'

She hated him. He was making her laugh—she could feel it bubbling up. And she did not want to laugh. 'You're outrageous, Ashthorpe!' she snapped, while wondering if to make her laugh was his way of easing what for her had been mightily mortifying.

'Pose for me?' he asked nicely, and she realised he had no personal interest in her body but was again seeing her with his artist's eye.

'I thought you only did portraits?' she stayed there to query. 'I presume you weren't thinking of painting my portrait?'

'I was thinking, in your case, I could quite enjoy painting nudes,' he answered charmingly, and she was hard put to it not to laugh.

Her lips did actually start to twitch. She turned sideways to him, but, since she had formed an opinion that he missed little, she doubted he had missed that he had reached her sense of humour.

'Goodnight, Mr Ashthorpe,' she bade him.

'Goodnight, fair maid,' he answered. She closed her door on him. She had a smile on her face.

When later she climbed into bed and put out the light she still had a smile on her face. Magnus was home; all was right with her world.

It was her curiosity—why had Magnus come back last night?—that had Taye getting out of bed on Sunday morning hoping that he was up and about. He was, and had already been out to collect his choice of Sunday newspapers.

'Tea?' she called, on popping her head round the sitting room door. He was deeply absorbed in newsprint.

'Just had one, thanks,' he refused.

Taye went and made herself a drink and returned to the sitting room, wanting to talk while at the same time not wanting to interrupt his time of relaxation.

Magnus, however, settled it when, having finished the section that had been holding his interest, he put his paper to one side, looked across to where she was sitting, and asked, 'So, what do you want to talk about?'

'Am I so transparent?'

'I have a crystal ball,' he replied solemnly.

'It's a pity you didn't use it last night when you came

barging in—' She broke off, colouring, dismayed that she, not him, had brought the subject up. She took a steadying breath. 'Go on, say it!' she invited sharply.

'As in—how was I to know you hadn't gone to your party? As in—you usually lock the bathroom door. And how was I to know you were in there as naked as the—?'

'I didn't lock it,' she butted in quickly. 'I—er—kind of got the idea you wouldn't be home last night.'

Magnus looked interested. 'What gave you that idea?'

The fact that you went out carrying an overnight bag was something of a whacking clue. But she could hardly tell him she had been peeking behind the curtains. Or could she? 'I saw you with your overnight bag.' She decided on honesty.

Magnus looked at her for a few silent moments, but, to save her any more blushes, refrained from asking how she had managed to do that. Then, giving an exaggerated sigh, 'Can't a man take his dirty washing home to his mother without you making capital out of it?'

'Your mother lives near here?' Taye asked in surprise.

'She has to live somewhere.'

'We have a washing machine here.'

'I couldn't take advantage.'

'I wasn't offering!' Taye exclaimed. Sometimes he was more than outrageous. 'What are you doing living here when you have a mother living locally?' she went on to challenge.

'Love her dearly though I do, I haven't lived in my old home since I left to go to university,' Magnus informed her. And asked, 'Could you go back to your old home to live—to live with your mother?'

'Point taken,' Taye replied, and wished she had the same loving relationship it sounded as though Magnus had with his mother. 'So, what about Elspeth?' It seemed only fair that, since Magnus knew all about Julian and Damien, she should know something about his friends of the opposite sex, in this case Penelope and Elspeth. 'What about your lady-friends?' came blurting out before she could stop it.

Magnus stared at her in some surprise; she supposed it had come out sounding a bit blunt. 'You're not proposing I should take them my dirty laundry?'

Again she was torn between murder and humour. She gave him a speaking look. 'You know all about Damien and Julian,' she said reproachfully.

'You're not suggesting I kiss and tell, I hope?'

She supposed she was, really. 'Perish the thought!' she exclaimed warmly. 'I was just attempting to get us more flat-matey,' she excused, and could have hit him when he burst out laughing.

'I'm not really into girly confidences,' he told her. And, before she could get offended, 'If you've nothing else planned, I'll take you out for lunch.'

'You can't afford it,' she said without thinking.

'I didn't suggest I'd take you to Claridges,' he replied.

'Tell you what,' she countered, realising she would quite like to go out to lunch with him, 'I'll take you for a pie and a pint if you like.'

He looked at her warmly, a new kind of light in his eyes that she could not understand. 'Accepted,' he said quietly, then seemed to collect himself, and, glancing from her to the window, 'What do you know? Sunshine,' he remarked casually. 'I think I'll read my papers out in the garden. Give me a shout when you want to go.'

Taye later spent a good ten minutes checking through her wardrobe for something smart to wear. Absurd, she freely owned. Who dressed up to go down to the pub?

At ten past twelve, dressed in cotton trousers and a loose but fairly smart top, she went out into the garden— where Magnus was in conversation with Jane and Huw Davies, the couple from the top floor apartment, who had decided to take advantage of the sunny weather too.

'Ready to go?' Magnus queried on seeing her, getting to his feet.

They spent a few minutes in friendly conversation with their fellow tenants, then went back indoors. Taye waited while Magnus went to wash the newsprint off his hands, and had to own that never before had she felt this flut-ter—a sort of breathless excitement—at the thought of going down to the pub with someone.

Though in actual fact they had not made it as far as the sitting room door when the telephone started to ring. 'For you?' she queried, with a glance to the tall and good looking male by her side.

'Leave it?' he replied. Plainly, if Elspeth was going to ring him he considered she would do so on his mobile.

'It might be Hadleigh,' Taye said, going over to the phone, thinking that perhaps her mother may have men-tioned to him that she had phoned last night. 'Hello?' she queried, on picking up the phone.

'Taye?'

Just that one word, that one abrupt sound of her name, and Taye knew that it was her mother. 'Hello, Mother,' she replied, while wondering how much her parent wanted this time. Feeling very conscious that Magnus was within earshot, she strove hard to keep her tone light. 'What can I do for you?' she asked pleasantly, and mo-mentarily forgot all about Magnus at her mother's reply.

'It's your brother.'

'What's wrong with him?' Taye asked sharply.

'Nothing except that he's turned idle and deliberately awkward!' Greta Trafford replied waspishly.

Taye knew her brother, knew all of his goodnesses along with his few human failings. And idle and deliberately awkward was something he definitely was not.

'What do you mean, idle?' she asked bluntly, forgetful in that moment that Magnus was in earshot.

'He has decided not to go to work this lunchtime.'

'That's not Hadleigh!' Taye exclaimed. 'No way is that Hadleigh!' And, sensing her mother's devious hand in this somewhere, she almost bluntly asked what her mother had done to upset him. But Taye knew that to challenge was not the way to handle her mother. 'Something must have upset him.'

'I suppose it must have,' Greta Trafford agreed. 'He's in his room now, writing to the powers that be to tell them to not hold his Oxford place for him.'

'He's doing *what?*' Taye asked faintly.

'He has this peculiar idea that you can't afford to finance him. That—'

'You *told* him!' Taye accused. 'When I particularly asked you not to, you told him I intended to get a bank loan to fund him! How could you?' she demanded, starting to grow incensed. 'You know how sensitive, how proud—'

'Who do you think you're talking to?' her mother cut her off. And, to show she was not in the mood to hear any more of it, without more ado she put down the phone.

Taye was so angry she dialled the number straight back. 'I'd like to speak to Hadleigh, please,' she said, with what control she could find. And had the phone put down on her again. Angry and extremely upset, Taye put down her own phone—only then suddenly becoming aware of Magnus standing there watching her.

'Trouble?' he asked, just that one word, and Taye was much too agitated to dissemble.

'I need to get to Pemberton,' she replied, her brain racing. How to get there? It had to be before Hadleigh posted his letter. It had to be today.

Magnus did not argue. Did not say What about lunch? But, as though having gleaned all that he needed to know from what he had overheard, and as if recalling how she had said how difficult it was to get there at weekends, 'I'll take you,' he promptly offered.

Taye blinked at that. 'You haven't got a car!' she reminded him.

But even as she spoke Magnus was heading out of the door. 'I'll borrow one,' he said, and was gone.

And Taye was so concerned about her brother she was extremely grateful. She did not care what sort of a car he borrowed from one of his probably equally hard-up friends. Be it a clapped-out box on four wheels, as long as it got them to Pemberton before Hadleigh posted that letter that would ruin his chances she would be just so terribly grateful.

And grateful too that Magnus had not stopped to ask the whys and wherefores, to argue or to reason, but, on seeing her distress, had acted. Now that was what you called a wonderful kind of flat-mate.

CHAPTER SIX

TAYE was not left to fret over her brother for very long before Magnus was back. She was agitated enough to not move from her position at the dining room window, but was standing in front of it, looking up and down the road watching for Magnus, when a long, sleek and up-to-the-minute car glided to a halt outside.

At first she did not believe it could be Magnus, and her eyes widened in surprise to see that it was indeed him who got out from behind the steering wheel. All too plainly, while not too flush himself, her flat-share knew at least one person who was not as impecunious as he.

It was odd, Taye considered as she hurried out into the main hall so as not to waste another moment—and especially odd when she was feeling so het-up about Hadleigh—that she should absently notice that the hall table was clear. Obviously Mr M. A. Penhaligon had collected his mail. He could not be staying with the Davieses, surely, or they would have invited him to spend time in the garden with them earlier.

Just then, however, Magnus put his key in the outer door, and as Taye at the same time reached it Mr M. A. Penhaligon, whoever he was, went out from her mind.

'Let's go,' Magnus encouraged, and, feeling choked suddenly, Taye had nothing to say until she was beside him on the genuine leather seats. 'Some car!' she commented, trying to not think of her brother and how the postbox in the village was but a short bike ride away.

'It sometimes pays to have friends with a few pennies,' Magnus replied.

More than a few pennies, she would have said. 'You've driven this car before,' she observed.

'What makes you say that?'

Taye wasn't sure. 'You're handling it so effortlessly,' she replied.

'A car like this doesn't require a lot of handling.' Magnus shrugged.

There was silence in the car for a while, and her worries about Hadleigh were back. 'Your friend… He didn't mind lending you his car?' she asked, wanting to talk about anything to take her mind off the problem that awaited her in Pemberton.

'He doesn't know.'

'You stole it?' she cried in alarm.

'Not at all. He's—er.. away,' Magnus explained.

'Where did you get the key remote?'

'You were a detective in your former life, yes?'

'Where?' she insisted. She *was* desperate to get to Pemberton, but no so desperate that she could accept Magnus being charged with auto theft.

'His girlfriend gave it to me. Satisfied?'

'Would that be the same girlfriend who moved in when you moved out?'

'I see you're all there with your lemon drops,' Magnus replied lightly. Taye said nothing, but waited. And was rewarded when he relented. 'Actually, yes. Mick left his car keys behind when he—'

'I thought you said his name was Nick?'

'What *is* this?' Magnus asked shortly.

'I'm sorry,' she at once apologised. 'I suppose I'm trying to focus on anything but that which awaits when we get there.'

'The problem obviously concerns your brother.'

As he had noted 'obviously', there seemed little point in pretending otherwise. Particularly since Magnus had gone out of his way to borrow a car to help her.

'Hadleigh's on the point of withdrawing his university application. I need to get to him to try and make him see reason.'

'You think he'll listen?'

Taye wished she knew. 'He's proud, and as stubborn as blazes,' she replied.

'Would you like me to have a crack at him?' Magnus offered.

'Oh, no!' Taye exclaimed at once. 'This is my problem. I'll sort it. Please don't...'

'Pride must run in the family,' he commented, but thankfully, as though accepting that she wanted to keep away from the subject of what awaited her at the end of their journey, he said no more.

And all was silent in the vehicle for some while until, having mentally marshalled her arguments to Hadleigh to the limits of exhaustion anyway, Taye sought for something else to pin her thoughts on.

'How long has your friend been away?' she enquired casually.

'Ages. A month or more at least.'

That surprised her! 'Would that be before or after you came to flat-share with me?' she asked, and realised that Magnus had seen straight away where she was heading.

'He moved his girlfriend in and was then called away. And, no, his girlfriend did not go with him.'

'Which means, if she's not working, she is there during the day while you are working in your attic studio,' Taye reasoned. And, on a sudden thought, 'If he's away, your friend Nick-Mick Knight, which makes you no longer an unwanted third, why did you have to leave at all?'

'Precisely because he is away.' He was watching his driving. 'He's the jealous sort. Good friend though he is, he wouldn't want me sleeping there.'

'But it's okay for you to continue to work there?'

'Apart from the utter disloyalty to a friend you appear to think I'm capable of, you're suggesting I might take advantage at some time during the day?'

Taye was beginning to wish she had never got started on this. But something—and she was sure *she* was not the jealous sort, so piffle to that—something did not seem able to let it go. 'So far as I'm aware, hanky-panky is not a reserved night-time occupation,' she commented loftily.

And had Magnus glance her way, his glance speculative, before he answered mildly, 'But then, dear Taye, so far as *I* am aware, you are not the most qualified to know anything at all about hanky-panky, are you?'

He'd got her there. Taye decided to let the subject drop. What with one thing and another, she accepted that her head was more than a little on the fidget just then, her thinking perhaps a little muddled. But in any event she was certain her fidgeting at it had nothing to do with jealousy. For crying out loud, why would she be jealous?

She had more important things to worry about, that was for sure. Hadleigh was back in her head. Oh, he could not let this chance go by. He just could not. He had to have his chance at Oxford; he just had to.

How could their mother have told him about her intention to fund him? Taye fretted. It had been a foregone conclusion that he would dig his proud heels in. A foregone conclusion that he would refuse to allow her to finance him.

'We turn left just up ahead.' She suddenly found her voice as she recognised where they were. And later, as they pulled up on the drive of her substantial, but cold old home, 'I'm so grateful to you for borrowing this car and bringing me here, Magnus...'

'But?' he queried, able to read her without any problem, she realised.

'But I need to have what might be quite a lengthy private talk to Hadleigh.'

'You'd like me to stay in the car?'

'Not at all. Though would you mind if I deserted you and...?'

'Fate worse than death—left me with your dragon mother?'

'She's not such a terrible dragon.' Fingers crossed, Taye felt honourbound to defend her more often than not disagreeable mother.

'You do what you have to do,' Magnus invited. 'I'll fit in.'

Something stirred in Taye for him then. 'Oh, Magnus,' she said softly, and just had to lean over and kiss him. 'Sorry.' She backed away instantly, for all it had been nothing like the lingering kiss he had given her that time.

'Your emotions are all over the place just now,' Magnus excused, to her relief. 'Come on—you won't feel better until it's done.'

That was true. And she had to admit to be feeling all upset inside as she took Magnus into the house and introduced him to her elegant but today icy parent.

'Your car, Mr Ashthorpe?' she enquired of the expensive automobile parked outside the drawing room window.

'Magnus borrowed it when I said I wanted to come here,' Taye butted in.

Greta Trafford took that as foreseen. 'I knew it was too much to hope that my daughter would throw in her lot with anyone other than some penniless artist!' she commented offensively.

'Mother!' Taye cried, appalled. 'Magnus, I...' She turned to him, horrified—but only to see that, far from looking offended, as he clearly had a right to be, Magnus appeared more amused than anything.

'Why not go and find Hadleigh?' he suggested pleasantly.

'You...' She hesitated, such a protective feeling for him coming over her—almost as if she wanted to guard him against her mother.

'Go,' he instructed.

Taye turned to glance at her mother, and would normally have asked some polite kind of, Is Hadleigh in his room? question, but, after her mother's dreadful remark just now, Taye felt that even that politeness would stick in her throat. Without another word, hoping her brother was still in the house, she went looking for him.

She found him in his room. He was lying on his bed, staring unhappily at the ceiling. 'Taye!' he exclaimed when he saw her, and sat up smartly. 'Mother rang you!' he at once realised. 'She shouldn't have.' And, plainly knowing why his sister was there, 'I'm not going,' he declared mulishly.

'Oh, love!' she cried, going over and sitting on his bed beside him. 'You can't give up this splendid opportunity...'

'It's impossible,' he muttered glumly.

But just then, to prove to Taye that, whatever the circumstances, he still desperately wanted to take his university place, she spotted a letter propped up on his desk beneath the window. Had he been prepared to abandon all hope, that letter would be reposing in the postbox by now.

'It is not impossible,' she countered. 'There's no—'

'I'm not taking your money,' he cut in emphatically.

'I've already earmarked the money for you,' she told him, feeling more than a touch desperate.

'It's not on, Taye,' he replied, shaking his head. And, obviously having used some of the intelligence she knew he had, 'I've thought it all through, and there is no way I'm going to allow you to finance me.'

'But—'

'No. Save your breath,' he cut in. 'I appreciate your offer, I truly do. But it won't stay at just that, will it?'

'It will, and it will only be for a few years, and—'

'And during those years Mother will still be on to you for help when the electricity bill or the phone bill comes in—or any other bill she hasn't put the money aside for. She's already hinted that she would expect me to send money home from any work I'm able to get in Oxford—and she's not above asking for some of my student loan. Which, with her constant harping on, apart from having to repay any money I've borrowed, would see me up to my eyes in debt years after I've got my degree—with no guarantee that I'll be able to get a halfway decent job afterwards to start repaying it.'

'I'll help. You know I—'

'No.' She had never known him so decisive. 'It's marvellous of you to offer, but, since I have no intention of saddling myself with debt for years and years to come—and I know in advance Mother will expect me to give her financial support when I start on the first rung of my career—I'm not saddling you with years and years of debt either.'

It was a long speech for him, her shy brother. But it

showed Taye the maturity of his thinking. She wished then that, bearing in mind the not unsubstantial allowance their mother received by their father's arrangement, she and her brother had the strength to tell their mother no when she demanded as her right financial aid from them too.

But, a kind of emotional blackmail though it was, Taye knew she, and Hadleigh too, were unable to turn a deaf ear to their mother's 'requests' for help with some bill or other.

'Hadleigh, listen to me…' Taye began.

Fifteen minutes later, having tried and tried anyhow to get through to him how very important this decision was to his whole life, she had to face that it was to no avail. He would have none of it; there was no way he would agree to her subsidising him. And in the end, while he remained resolutely determined that she was not going to finance his time at Oxford, Taye saw that her only hope of getting him to change his mind lay in her trying to think up something that would be more acceptable to him than, as he put it, that she should beggar herself on his behalf.

'I'll think of something,' she told him urgently, panicking madly with not the smallest idea of what that something might be. 'Just promise me you won't post that letter until I've had a chance to think.'

'There is no way,' he stated. 'If there was a way I could go without being a burden to you, I'd leap at it. But there isn't. You know it and I know it.'

'But there's no need to send that letter yet,' she argued. 'You've five or six weeks yet before you get your exam results. So there's no earthly reason for you to do anything until then.'

Hadleigh did not look convinced, but to her relief did

see the logic of her argument. 'I'll hold off until I've got my A level results,' he promised at last. And, while Taye would have preferred a promise that he would accept his Oxford place when offered, at least with his promise not to send that letter just yet she had some time to try and think up something.

'And you'll phone me first, before you do anything at all? Promise?' Taye asked.

'Persistent to the last,' he commented, but smiled as he said, 'I promise.'

'Good. Now, come and say hello to Magnus. He borrowed a car to drive me down.'

'Oh, Taye, I've put you and Magnus to so much trouble.'

'That's what sisters are for,' she told him lightly.

'And flat-mates,' he took up as they left his room.

Her mother was alone in the drawing room when they went in. 'Where's Magnus?' Taye asked, with a hasty glance to the drawing room window. Relief sped in. The car was still there. For a moment or two she had thought that he'd had enough of her mother and had decided to return to London—alone.

'He's in the garden. Apparently the colours of the mixed geraniums are quite spectacular.'

'He's an artist,' Hadleigh exclaimed warmly.

'You did mention,' his mother replied dryly, causing Taye to wonder if Hadleigh had been singing her flat-share's praises since he had been taken for a pint by him a couple of weeks ago, when he'd been so upset.

'I'll go and see him,' Taye murmured, and escaped into the grounds of the house.

She saw Magnus before he saw her—and her heart turned over. She did not need to analyse the sudden rush of feeling for him that crashed in with a mighty roar—

but accepted what had been there in front of her a short while ago when, sitting in the car, he had bade her, 'You do what you have to do. I'll fit in.' and she had just had to kiss him. She accepted then what that protective feeling she had experienced had all been about for this man who had no need of anyone's protection. She was totally and irrevocably in love with him!

Feeling utterly all at sea from her discovery, Taye just then realised that while Magnus might not have seen her, he knew she was there. 'Everything fixed?' he asked, and that was before he turned around.

Taye went forward, still catching her breath but hoping to hide the love in her eyes, hoping that her voice would sound normal. 'Hadleigh has written a letter that will end his chances if he posts it. I've managed to get him to promise not to send it for a while.' She smiled at Magnus. 'Er—how did it go with you?'

'Me?' he asked, as if he had no idea what she was talking about.

'Was my mother too awful?' she asked, the time gone for pretence.

'Thoroughly awful,' he replied pleasantly—she had guessed as much; why else would he seek refuge in the garden? 'How old did you say you were when you left home?'

She did not remember having said. 'Twenty. Three years ago,' she answered honestly, and loved him yet more when he forbore to say he wondered how she had managed to stay until she was twenty.

'Ready to go back?' he asked instead.

'When you are,' she replied, not wanting to inflict any more of her mother's acid on him.

Not that they saw Greta Trafford again. She had left the drawing room when they went in, in favour of her bedroom. Taye knew she would not wish to be disturbed. Hadleigh came out to the drive with them and admired the car, but grinned at Magnus as he commented, 'By contrast, I'd better get out my bike. I do some waiting work in a restaurant,' he explained to Magnus. 'I rather let them down at lunchtime.'

'Did you let them know you wouldn't be in?' Magnus asked.

'Oh, yes. I wouldn't just not turn up.'

'Then I'm sure they'll forgive you.' Magnus too grinned. 'If you go now I'm also sure they'll let you help with a bit of dishwashing.'

Hadleigh's grin had widened as the two shook hands, the man she loved and the brother she loved, and Magnus opened the passenger door for her. 'You haven't eaten!' Taye exclaimed as the car gently rolled its way back down the drive. 'I promised you a pie and a pint! I'm sorry,' she apologised at once. 'I forgot all about it when my mother phoned. Would you like to stop somewhere on the way…?'

'You haven't eaten either.'

'I'm not hungry. But you…'

'We'll get something when we get home,' Magnus suggested, and that sounded so pretty wonderful to her— home, their home—that she temporarily forgot that she should be setting her mind to other things. For one, how on earth was she to get Hadleigh to take his place at university when he was so stubbornly refusing to let her chip in financially?

But if that ever present problem had been sidelined under the mammoth discovery that the man by her side held her whole heart, the problem had not been sidelined by that man, she realised.

For barely had they driven another mile than he was asking, 'Feeling better now?'

'Less panicky, do you mean?'

'Does your mother always wind you up?'

Taye had not really thought about it, but she had suddenly given her first loyalty to this man she loved, and wanted only to be truthful with him. 'I rather think she does,' she admitted.

'Then it's just as well that you're living with a penniless artist,' he said nicely, and when she glanced at him, looking for a sting, she saw none. And she loved him some more that he was only trying to lighten what had been a tense time for her. That he was as good as saying that he was on her side.

Her thoughts alternated between him and Hadleigh for the rest of that drive. With Magnus sitting next to her, sitting this close, it was so heady she was having the utmost difficulty in concentrating for any length of time solely on her brother.

She concluded she must abandon serious thought until she was on her own, Magnus not there. Then she would try to work something out. Though what escaped her.

'Something on toast? Or shall I see what's in the freezer?' she enquired when, five minutes after arriving home, they met in the kitchen.

'Would your mother really allow you to take out a bank loan to fund Hadleigh?' he asked, which was no sort of an answer in Taye's opinion.

Though, since he had been within earshot when she had grown angry enough not to care who heard her side of that telephone conversation when her mother had rung, Taye supposed she could not blame him for asking the question he had. The only wonder was that he had waited this long to put it. Though, as he had observed in the car, her emotions had been all over the place, so perhaps that was why he had left it until now.

'Oh, yes.' She answered his question. 'I'm afraid she would.'

Magnus nodded at that, but went on to ask another question, one which she just had not given thought to. 'So why, when you had asked her to not tell him what you proposed to do, would she deliberately make sure that he knew?'

Taye stared at Magnus. 'I—don't know,' she answered slowly, while she hurriedly searched round for a reason that she had not previously so much as considered. She had thought it might be all part and parcel of her mother not being happy unless she was upsetting someone. But, apart from the satisfaction she would gain from seeing them all jump through hoops, what else would she gain? 'Not unless she's anxious not to lose the amount Hadleigh puts into the coffers now. But she knows that I'll help out if she gets into any sort of financial difficulty.'

'You do so now?' he asked.

He was too shrewd by far, in her opinion. 'Er—not so much,' she prevaricated. 'Anyhow, my father has seen to it that she has a splendid allowance.'

'But it's never enough?'

It would never be enough. Taye knew that as fact. Were that allowance to be doubled then Greta Trafford would still want more. 'I don't suppose it's any too easy for her,' Taye replied, her loyalty stretched, but feeling a shade uncomfortable at the thought of running her mother down. Even to Magnus, the man she loved.

Whether he noticed that she was not feeling too comfortable with the subject she did not know, but he abruptly left the matter of her mother and her grasping ways to enquire, 'What about your father?'

Taye blinked, not at all with him. 'What about my father?'

'Are you going to ring him?'

'What about?'

'This latest development.'

'I can't do that!' she gasped, horrified at the very idea.

'Why not?'

She stared at Magnus. He did not understand. 'Because I can't.'

Magnus stared back at her, all male and logical. 'He sounds an honourable man...' he began.

'He *is* an honourable man!' Taye flew. Love Magnus though she did, she was not going to sanction anyone thinking less of her father. But, in the face of Magnus calmly observing her, taking in the twin spots of colour in her cheeks, she calmed down a little to explain. 'He will have to know that Hadleigh has decided to not accept any university place offered...'

'Like you had to decide not to,' Magnus put in, his expression gentle.

She found his gentle look unnerving, and guessed then that her emotions must still be to some degree all over the place. 'I knew long before I was eighteen that university was out,' she said quickly.

'What did your father have to say about that?' Magnus insisted, and she could only look at him and wonder at his 'dog with a bone' tenacity to find out her father's involvement in the decision making when it came to his two offspring.

'If you must know—' she replied, more sharply than she meant—not that it appeared to bother Magnus how sharply she spoke, because he stayed in there, leaning against one of the kitchen units as he waited for her answer. 'If you must know,' she repeated, 'I let my father believe I'd gone off the idea of going to university.'

'You lied to him?'

'Oh, shut up,' she mumbled. But, after some silent seconds, felt forced to admit, 'Yes, I suppose I did. But what else was I to do? He had given my mother the house and every penny he could spare. He didn't have anything else to give.'

'And your mother wanted you earning, not studying.' It was not a question; it was a statement.

'How did you get to be so perceptive? I thought you were an artist not some wised-up brainbox!'

'You'd be amazed what we artists see,' he informed her. But was apparently still not ready to let go what she guessed was his opinion that her father should be told when he went on, 'So—you're not going to tell your father that his son, too, is going to be denied his chance—and why?'

'I can't!' she exclaimed warmly, and, suddenly not wanting to fall out with Magnus, 'Don't you see? It is precisely because my father is an honourable man that I cannot tell him.' And, realising that perhaps she should explain, 'My father has met someone—a very nice lady. She's a teacher,' Taye began. 'His years with my mother were not happy years. In fact, knowing him as I do, I can only now wonder that he tolerated living at home for as long as he did. But now he is about to find happiness with Hilary. Only I know in advance that, were I to tell him that financial hardship is the reason for Hadleigh turning his back on a university education, my father would straight away cancel all his plans to remarry.'

'Because?'

'Because he would see any further financial help he

was able to give us as depriving his new wife of what is rightfully hers. Or, worse, he would see his new and salary-earning wife as making a financial contribution to something that is his responsibility alone. And he would not be able to accept that.'

'But he would accept you impoverishing yourself to take out a bank loan?'

He wouldn't know. 'I wouldn't tell him!' Taye exclaimed. 'He'd have a fit if—' She broke off. There was a sudden stillness about Magnus that caused her to know that his perceptive artist's brain had just seen something else. 'What...?' she began.

'Presumably, until your mother's phone call today, you were all set to go for that bank loan?'

'I may still go that route if I can think up some way to convince Hadleigh that I'm—er—not, to use your word, "impoverishing" myself. He's so proud—'

'I don't mean to be prying,' Magnus cut her off, 'but...'

'You've done nothing but pry ever since we got home!' she protested.

'We're flat-mates; we can share everything,' he explained, and she had to smile. Though she was not smiling a moment later, and nor was he when, 'Forgive me for knowing that, financially, you struggle to keep your head above water...' he said, managing to look as though, with the bit once more between his teeth, it would be just the same if she forgave him or didn't. 'But how did you anticipate repaying any loan your bank made you?'

No! No, she did not want to tell him! She loved him— loved him so much she could not bear to live apart from him. She wanted to stay living with him. Yet she knew if she were able to carry through her original plan that she was going to have to live elsewhere.

She looked away from him, her glance absently taking in the stove. 'You haven't eaten!' she said in a diverting rush. 'You've missed lunch, and—'

'How, Taye?' He refused to be diverted. 'I imagine that would be one of the first questions your bank would ask before considering making you any sort of a loan. How are you going to repay it?'

She opened her mouth to tell him, and could not. She closed it again. But he was waiting. She had intended to tell him anyway. Only she had not faced then that he had stolen her heart.

'I...' Her voice was suddenly all husky...guiltily, painfully, in love with him husky. 'I was going to—move into somewhere smaller—somewhere cheaper,' she managed to drag out from between reluctant lips.

Magnus eyed her solemnly for long, tortuous seconds. 'You were going to leave here? Leave this apartment?'

'I didn't want to. You know how I love it here,' she said. 'But I couldn't see I had any other choice.'

'I see,' Magnus commented tautly. But a tough note had entered his tones as he determinedly challenged, 'Do I assume, as the other half of this flat-share, that you intended to tell me about it some time?' Oh, crumbs. 'Or was I just expected to come home one evening and find you'd done a flit, bag and baggage gone?'

'No!' she exclaimed. 'I would have told you...'

'When?' he demanded. 'Before or after...?'

'Don't! Oh, don't Magnus,' she pleaded. 'I wanted to tell you, only—' she broke off. How could she tell him that she had not been able to mention it because she had been too busy falling in love with him—only she had not known about that herself then? 'Oh, please don't...' she cried huskily, and, unable to look at him, stared down at the floor.

And the next she knew, whether because of something in her look or maybe in her tone she neither knew nor cared just then, Magnus had left his position by the kitchen units and had come over to her. And his voice was all soft and bone-meltingly gentle when he gathered her into his arms in an empathy of the moment and sympathetically breathed, 'Poor little love, you've been on an emotional merry-go-round all day. You've had enough, haven't you?' he murmured. 'You've got as much grief as you can handle without me badgering away at you.'

'I was going to t-tell you.'

'Shh, and let me give you a hug.'

In seventh heaven, she leaned against him. Soon he would take his arms from around her—and she wanted to savour every delicious moment.

She put her arms around his waist, and felt him drop a light comforting kiss to the top of her head. Her arms, of their own volition, it seemed to her, tightened about him, and she raised her head and looked up into warm grey eyes.

'Don't look at me like that unless you mean it,' he murmured.

'Look at you how?' she answered huskily, just the fact of looking into his warm and gentle gaze sending any thinking power haywire.

'As though you want to be—kissed,' he replied, but made no move to release her from his hold.

She smiled a dreamy kind of smile. 'I think I might like to be kissed,' she invited softly, her dreamy smile deepening as she added, 'If memory serves, you do it so nicely.'

He gave a low laugh, and his head came down. He did not wait for a second invitation, but tenderly placed his mouth over hers.

'Ooh,' she whispered, when he drew back to look into her eyes once more. 'That was so nice—do you think I could have another?'

'I don't think...' he began, his eyes searching her face. Then a kind of groan escaped him, and the next Taye knew was that she was being drawn closer up against him, and his kiss this time, as well as giving, was taking.

'Magnus!' She sighed his name.

'Magnus, no?' he enquired.

She kissed him, stretched up and, with her body leaning against him, kissed him. 'What do you think?' she asked shyly.

He looked into her lovely blue eyes, his eyes showing delight. He kissed her—with growing warmth. And Taye, her heart pounding against her ribs, responded fully.

For how long they stood in the kitchen, their bodies pressed up against each other as they kissed, and held, and kissed, gave and took, and then kissed some more, Taye could not have said. All she knew was that to be in his arms like this was bliss—pure bliss.

When next Magnus pulled back she saw a fire there in his wonderful grey eyes that, feeling slightly incredulous, she realised she was responsible for lighting.

She guessed that her eyes must be showing pretty much that same fire, because as Magnus looked tenderly down at her, kissed first one corner of her mouth and then the other, he smiled, and said, 'I think, Miss Trafford, that, in answer to your question, we would both be more comfortable elsewhere.'

Taye was ready to agree with whatever he suggested. And she guessed he must have read that in her eyes too. Because when next his mouth sought hers, he at the same time lifted her up in his arms—and kissed her all the way to her bedroom.

He did not set her down again until he was standing next to her bed. Gently then he kissed her, his tongue teasing at her slightly parted lips.

'Oh, Magnus!' she cried, and gripped on to him tightly.

'Sweet Taye,' he murmured, his hands gently exploring beneath the fine material of her loose top. With breath-holding torture, as his hands searched unhurriedly upwards, she clung on to him. And gave a gasp of pure wanting when finally those caressing hands took possession of her full and throbbing breasts. 'You can say no any time you want to,' he thought to gently state, perhaps bearing in mind her inexperience.

'What a diabolical suggestion,' she whispered, and loved him some more when he laughed a low, tender laugh.

Again they kissed, and the fire inside her began to burn out of control when, her bra somehow undone, Taye felt the warmth of his hands on the creamy skin of her breasts, cupping and moulding.

'I want to get close to you,' she murmured shyly, for her words sounded forward in her ears.

'Do what feels right for you,' he instructed softly.

'May I unbutton your shirt?'

'I would love you to unbutton my shirt,' he replied lightly. And her heart swelled with her love for him. But her fingers were shaky as they neared the buttons. 'Nervous, darling?' Magnus asked, his hands leaving her breasts to take hold of her hands.

'A—bit,' she owned, her heart melting at that endearment. She knew, though, that she had no need to be nervous. To make love with Julian had not been right for her—because she did not love Julian. But she loved Magnus with her whole heart, and to make love with him was right for her.

'Am I going too fast for you?'

She shook her head, and, to prove it, set about unbuttoning his shirt. Magnus helped her. And—removed it. 'Oh!' she whispered huskily, and just had to gaze at his magnificent broad chest. Just had to touch him. Touch the dark hair, his skin, his nipples. She felt his spontaneous movement and, her eyes wide, she looked up. 'I'm sorry,' she apologised. And asked, 'Do you mind me— er—exploring you like this?'

'Sweet love,' he replied. 'It's all new to you, isn't it?' But, to show that he did not mind in the least, he hauled her into his arms once more, and all was silent as they kissed, and held, and kissed.

Taye, without panic, became aware that Magnus was removing her top. Then removing her bra. She was still not panicking when, in next to no time, they were both standing naked down to the waist. Why would she panic? She loved him, he was her love.

But as Magnus looked down, so instinctively her hands shot to cover her breasts. He smiled gently, his eyes tender with understanding. But, drawing her to him, he kissed her with such a growing passion that she forgot all about modestly hiding her intimate self from him and wrapped her arms around him—her naked breasts pressed up against his naked chest as she tried to get closer, yet closer to him.

And this time when he relaxed his hold and looked down to her breasts her hands stayed where they were, resting on his shoulders. 'You're exquisite,' he breathed, and just had to bend his head to salute in turn each hardened pink tip of her breasts, his lips lingering to pleasure and tease. A thrill of pure desire swept through her.

But when she found that, without apparent haste, Magnus had moved her, moved with her, until they were both lying on her bed, unwanted nerves returned and began to bite with a vengeance.

She wanted to make love with Magnus. It felt so right to make love with him. And yet… A gasp left her as with gentle seeking hands his fingers strayed inside her trousers, investigating parts of her where no man had trespassed before.

'Magnus!' she cried out.

His hand stilled. 'I didn't mean *now!*' he groaned.

'What?' She barely knew where she was, and had no idea what he was talking about.

'I said you could say no at any time, but I didn't mean for you to say no at this late stage,' he enlightened her, having picked up, from the way she had cried his name, it seemed, that at almost the point of no return she was unsure. 'You know I want you?' he asked gruffly.

Yes, she knew that. She was not so innocent that she did not know that. She wanted him too—but she also wanted, needed, him to tell her that he loved her—even if it wasn't true. Which, of course, it wasn't.

'You're saying no now, right?' he asked, a note of strain there in his voice somewhere.

Tell me you love me! Just one word of love, that was all she would ask. But no word of love had been spoken. 'This—this isn't right,' she said chokily. 'I'm—confused,' she confessed. Wasn't that the truth!

She wanted to make love with him, was quite desperate to know his body, to love him with her body—and knew, weakly, that should he care to he could so easily persuade her that it *was* right.

But Magnus was not into persuading, apparently. As though the feel of her warm belly beneath his touch burned his skin, he yanked his hand away and sat up, his back to her so he should not see her uncovered breasts.

And, as if needing to focus his thoughts on something other than her, until a few minutes ago, eager and waiting, wanting body, 'I'd better go and take that car back!' he grunted, and, grabbing up his shirt as he went, he strode urgently from her room.

CHAPTER SEVEN

MAGNUS did not come home that night. And Taye felt that she loved and hated him at one and the same time. Not that she was ready to see him again yet; the way she felt now she did not know if she would ever be ready to see him again. But jealousy scourged her; just who was he spending the night with?

She tried to think that after he had returned the car he had borrowed he had gone on to his mother's home. But the name Elspeth, Elspeth, Elspeth insisted on hammering away in her head.

Taye tried to think of Hadleigh and what she must do about his refusal to accept her help. But all too soon she found she was again thinking of Magnus—and his lips on hers.

His kisses were sensational, his caresses so tender. He could have been hers, she his, for a short while. She felt so mixed up she did not know whether she was glad or sorry that their lovemaking had ended when it had. Indeed, now that she had space to think about it, she could barely remember how she had caused their lovemaking to come to such an abrupt end.

She had loved his endearments, she recalled. The way he had murmured her name, called her 'darling'. Had she truly heard him call her 'sweet love'? It was all such heady stuff, she could no longer be sure. But what she was sure of was that, though he may have called her 'sweet love', no other word of love had left his lips.

Perhaps all women wanted to be told that they were

loved that first time. She did not know. All she knew was that he had not told her he loved her. And he did not love her. And he never would. And he had probably spent the night with Elspeth—and Taye hated him.

She felt bleary-eyed when she went in to work the next day, but was too busy to dwell overlong on that which really mattered to her—how was she going to face Magnus again, and what was she going to do about her brother?

Julian Coombs stopped by her desk during the afternoon. 'Good weekend?' she asked, finding a smile, glad she had managed to remember he had been at some rally or other.

'It would have been better with you there,' he answered. She made no comment—she just wasn't up to this. 'Doing anything tonight?' he asked.

'I'm a bit up to my eyes at the moment,' she hedged.

'I've got to go to our Edinburgh branch again tomorrow. But I'll be back Friday,' he said, and pressed, 'Come out with me Friday?'

Taye knew then that this could not go on, though she was loath to say what she must at the office. 'I—rather wanted a word with you,' she brought out, after an internal struggle, only to see him start to look a little wary.

'I rather wanted a word with you too,' he said solemnly.

Please say the word you wanted is that you've met somebody else, that you're just being kind and want to dump me as nicely as you can. Oh, please do. 'I'll see you on Friday, then,' she agreed, knowing that the office was just not the place for either of them to bid the other a social farewell.

Magnus tried to get to toehold within a very short space of Julian leaving her desk. She pushed Magnus out of her thoughts and made valiant efforts to concentrate solely on her work.

But when the time came to go home she fell to wondering if he would be there when she got there. Did she want to see him? Well, of course she wanted to see him; she loved the wretched man. But... Taye decided to work an extra hour or so.

But a half-hour later she could stay away no longer, and cleared her desk ready for a fresh start in the morning.

Her heart started to hurry up its beat the nearer she got to the apartment she shared with him. She tried turning her thoughts away from him. Now, what on earth was she going to do about Hadleigh?

Taye was no nearer to finding an answer to that problem when from the top of the street where the apartment was situated she saw someone standing outside of her building. He was vaguely familiar. It was... Surely not! Her feet went from walking to hurrying. 'Dad!' she exclaimed when she was near enough for him to hear her. He had never been to the flat before. 'What are you doing here?'

'Trying to get in,' he answered dryly.

She grinned. 'Come in,' she invited, unlocking the outer door. She guessed before she opened the flat door that Magnus was not home yet—if indeed he intended coming home. Otherwise he would have answered the intercom and, as he had with Hadleigh, he would have asked her father in.

'Nice place,' Alden Trafford approved as Taye took him into the sitting room.

Taye sensed he had not come to town merely to admire where she now lived. 'Take a seat. I'll make some tea,' she said, her thoughts darting all over the place.

In normal circumstances her father would have phoned in advance if he intended paying her a call, she felt sure. So she could only imagine something out of the norm had taken place. She did so hope that everything was all right with him and Hilary and that he had not hit some snag with his divorce.

'What's up, Dad?' she asked as she handed him a cup of tea.

He did not preamble but came straight out and told her, 'I had lunch with your brother today.' And, while Taye was still blinking at that, 'Oh, love. I got it all wrong, didn't I? And you're the one who had to pay.'

He sounded so upset Taye could not bear it. 'I'm fine,' she assured him, having no idea what had caused him to be so grief-stricken.

'You should have told me,' he mourned. 'I should have pressed you further. Blindly, when I full well know your mother could lie for England, I believed every word she told me. Believed what you told me. But I should never have left you with her. I see that now. I just thought then, and when I know her so well too, that she was the better person to look after you. I thought I was doing what was best for you.'

Taye knew that. How could he have taken her and Hadleigh with him when he had split from her mother? He had barely had a roof over his own head back then. But she still could not make much sense of why he had come, or what it was he was saying. Though, from what he had said so far, Taye saw her mother at the root of his visit somewhere. 'This has something to do with my mother?' she asked—and, oh, my word if she did!

'Your mother rang me last night to inform me that Hadleigh had decided not to go to Oxford.'

'Oh, she didn't! Oh, I'm so sorry. I didn't want to worry you or—' Taye began fretfully.

'Then you should have!' Alden Trafford cut in severely. But lost his severe look to say more gently, 'I'm your father, Taye. It's my place to be worried when things go wrong.'

'But you're getting married, and I didn't want—'

'I think I know you well enough now to know why you have done what you have. But, had you come to me, I could have sorted everything out.'

'You could?' she asked, respecting him, but doubting he could sort this one out. But how much did he know? Did he know why Hadleigh had made the decision he had?

'I could,' her father confirmed. 'And you needn't be scared of telling me too much. I know everything.'

Taye stared at him, uncertain still. 'You and Hilary… This—um…'

'This will make not the slightest difference to our plans,' Alden Trafford assured her. 'And I know what you intended to do for Hadleigh—had he let you.'

'He told you?'

'I know he turned stubborn when his mother told him you intended to go around barefoot in order to secure a loan—and how he refused to let you do it.'

'Barefoot's a bit of an exaggeration,' Taye said with a smile, hurrying on, when her father did not return her smile, 'I just wanted to do whatever I could to help.'

'And I appreciate that. Taye. But it's not your place to do that; it's mine. And,' he said heavily, 'it has all been taken care of.'

Taye stared at her father. His needs were small, but so was his income. She doubted that there was anything over for much else. 'Mother shouldn't have phoned you...' she began, but only to be contradicted.

'Somebody should, and it wouldn't have been you. And, after speaking to Hadleigh today, it's a foregone conclusion that he wasn't going to ring.'

'Don't worry, Dad. I'll see he gets his chance somehow,' she said, starting to get seriously worried.

'You don't have to. I've told you, everything has been taken care of.'

'It—has?'

'Your mother said when she rang last night that Hadleigh had decided against university. That said, she went on to stress how, being a six-footer like me, and big with it, he takes a man size in all his clothes and shoes and she just couldn't keep up. And I,' he said, shaking his head, 'almost swallowed it. In fact it wasn't until I was relating all this to Hilary that I realised that what Greta had said had a very familiar ring. It was, in fact, an almost word-for-word playback of the telephone call I had from her when you were sixteen and I discussed with her about you going to university when you were old enough.' He looked at her sorrowfully then. 'The decision not to go was your mother's, not yours, wasn't it?' he asked.

In the face of such a point blank question, Taye could not lie to him. 'We couldn't afford for me to go,' she mumbled.

And looked at her father, staggered, when he said bluntly, 'Yes, we could,' and went on to explain, 'A month after you were born I set up a fund especially so that, should we reach hard times—though Lord knows I never expected to—there would be a pot of money available to pay for your education. I set up the same sort of fund when Hadleigh was born.'

'I never knew that!' Taye exclaimed in awe.

'Foolishly, I see now, I didn't want my children to concern themselves about money. But hindsight's a wonderful thing—it's now plain to me that I should have told you. I was, in fact, going to tell Hadleigh. I thought I'd wait until he rang to tell me his A level results, and tell him then. Anyhow, that's by the way now. When things went rocky for me financially I had to move to freeze that education fund. But there would still have been enough when you reached eighteen to see you didn't have to worry about money. I'm afraid, my dear, that all your mother wanted was the money that was set aside for your further education.'

'Oh!' Taye gasped, knowing without question that her mother had had that money, and spent it. Then something suddenly clicked. 'Mother knew all about those funds from day one, didn't she?' she exclaimed.

'That's right.' Her father was right up there with her. 'Money has always been like a god to her. She worships the stuff, and was after Hadleigh's education fund too. And I nearly missed seeing it! But no more,' he said decisively. 'Over the years that woman has bled me dry. But *I* have taken as much as I'm prepared to take. From now on I shall take charge of finances. You, young lady, are not to give her any more. Yes, I know all about that. I'm afraid I caught Hadleigh at a weak moment over lunch. He was very down to start with, but after I'd explained about his fund, and how he was to have his chance, he opened up to me.'

'He's all right?' Taye asked, concerned.

'Never better. I told him I was coming here. He said to give you a big hug and a thank-you. I did ask him to come back with me to Warwickshire, to come and live with me, but he wants to be around to pick up his exam results, and he has his job and other loose ends he wants to deal with before October. Though I think he's ready to spend time with me during his student vacations.'

'Will Mother mind?'

'It's not her fault that she just doesn't have that maternal instinct, I suppose. But as to whether she'll mind...' He smiled suddenly. 'To quote Rhett, ''Frankly, my dear, I don't give a damn.'' I've told her not to bother you or Hadleigh for money, and that if she's that hard up she can sell that big house. With the price it would fetch she'd have enough to purchase at least two very respectable properties and still be able to live comfortably on what's left over.'

'Will—?' Taye began, and then heard Magnus's key in the door. 'That will be my flat-share,' she broke off to tell her father. And was glad his glance went to the door, because as Magnus came in so she blushed scarlet. 'Hello, Magnus,' she said in a rush, aware of his eyes flitting from her visitor and then staying with her fading colour. 'Come and say hello to my father.' She then went on to introduce the two men.

'I seem to know your face,' her father commented. 'Have we met before?'

'I'm sure not. I think I must have ''one of those faces,''' Magnus replied easily, as the two men shook hands.

In Taye's view he definitely did not have 'one of those faces'. He was much too good-looking, for one thing— though she did recall that Damien Fraser had seemed to think he knew Magnus from somewhere. But all that was forgotten as Magnus and her father exchanged one or two comments, and then her father was remarking that it was time he was off.

'But I haven't given you anything to eat!' Taye protested. 'You can't go without—'

'I had a huge banquet of a meal with Hadleigh at lunchtime,' Alden Trafford replied. And, smiling, 'I did phone Hilary earlier, but she'll be anxious to hear more.'

He and Magnus shook hands again, and Taye went out into the hall with her father. 'I'm still trying to take in your good news,' she said, and was on the receiving end of a warm hug.

'I wish there was some way I could make it up to you. When I think…' He shook his head regretfully.

'Oh, please don't! I think it's been harder for you than for me.'

'I doubt that,' he said solemnly, but was smiling as Taye hugged him back and asked him to give her best to Hilary.

Taye returned to the apartment half wishing that Magnus had gone to his room. He had not, but was still in the sitting room. And she was glad that he had not disappeared—loving him was turning her sane world on its head.

'Your father had lunch with Hadleigh?' Magnus commented, and she just had to smile.

'What you don't know, find out. Not that you're one to pry, of course.'

'So?'

'So my mother rang my father last night to tell him that Hadleigh did not want to go to university. Basically, Dad smelt a rat, and went to Pemberton today, took Hadleigh out to lunch, and informed him that he had made financial provision for his adult education when Hadleigh was a baby. I gather that by the pudding stage my brother was back on course to go to Oxford.'

Magnus took that on board in no seconds flat, and

was all too soon there with his summing up. 'Do I gather that the same provision he made for you went where Hadleigh's allocated finances were likely to go?'

This man Ashthorpe was too sharp for his own good! 'Brainy as well as good-looking!' she commented, with what was supposed to be acid.

'I cannot deny it,' he sighed. She turned away so he should not see her lips tugging upwards. But quickly turned back when, as sharp as she had thought, he added, 'I take it you now have no need to look for less expensive accommodation?'

Taye stared at him transfixed. She had not got that far in her thinking. But joy entered her heart. 'There's no need now, is there?' she answered, her voice strangely husky. She was having the greatest difficulty in holding in a beam of a smile that might have given him some indication of how she did not want to leave the apartment and now, more particularly, Magnus himself.

But all at once she noticed that his expression had gone to look deadly serious. 'You're not afraid, Taye?' he asked gravely.

'Afraid?' The only fear she had was that he would see just why she was so delighted they did not now have to part.

'I shouldn't have kissed you yesterday,' he said as pink seared her cheeks. And, while taking in her heightened colour, he was determined, it appeared, to give the subject the airing he seemed to think was required. 'You were in a vulnerable and emotional state before I kissed you. I should—'

'You didn't take advantage, if that's what you're thinking!' she exclaimed, not happy to be discussing what had happened, but too honest to let him take the blame when it had been she who had so loved that first kiss, and had

pushed for a second. 'I was perfectly willing—' nay, eager '—about—about what went on. I wanted... Only...
Only...' She ran out of steam.

Thankfully he seemed sufficiently convinced to let it
go. He smiled suddenly. And as swiftly as he had got
onto that subject he changed it. 'I'm having a coffee.
Want one?'

In actual fact she didn't. The teacups were still on the
table from her father's visit. 'Yes, please,' she accepted,
and gave up wondering about the topsy-turvy world of
being in love.

It took her a long while to get to sleep that night, and
she thought it had very little to do with the caffeine in
the coffee. There was just so much to think about. She
did not wish to visualise the kind of conversation that
had gone on between her parents. Her father was slow to
anger, but when roused, Taye knew, would not back
down again.

She thought of Hadleigh. Leaving it as late as he could,
he had telephoned, his first words a fairly cautious, 'Have
you seen Dad?'

'I hear you had a banquet at lunch,' she had replied,
and listened while her ecstatic brother grew excited and
repeated more or less the same that their father had told
her. So much for Hadleigh not wanting to go to Oxford;
he could barely wait to get there.

So much too, for her having to try to work out something with regard to getting Hadleigh to accept her financial help. She would no longer have to do that. And, for
an added bonus, she did not have to find somewhere
smaller to live, and so leave the apartment—and Magnus.

Ah, Magnus! She thought about him. How could she
not? She thought of his smiles, his occasional laugh, the
way he made her laugh—whether she wanted to laugh or

not. She thought about his kisses, his tender caresses. She thought about him in all of his moods—and wondered how she had ever thought that she hated him. She eventually fell asleep, still thinking about him.

Taye still had Magnus in her head the next day. She was busy at her desk; then found she had drifted off to think of him again. At one time she might have banished him. This time she let him stay.

He went briefly from her head, though, when Damien Fraser, ever a trier, phoned. 'Are you still going out with that other bloke?' he asked.

'Yes,' she replied.

'Anyone I know?'

'No,' she said.

'Goodbye—no, *au revoir!*' he bade her.

'*Ciao,*' she responded, though goodbye just about covered it. And, with Magnus pushing Damien out of her head, she got on with some work.

Taye left her office early that night. She wanted to see Magnus. Not for any particular reason other than she had a need to see him. Much good did it do her! They passed in the hall—she coming in, he on his way out.

'Be late back!' he said in passing.

Good of you to come home at all! 'I won't wait up!'

He grinned. 'See you.'

Jealousy played havoc with her for the rest of the night. She was in bed—not sleeping—when her listening ears heard his key in the door. Half of her was glad Elspeth had kicked him out. The other half hated him that he had stayed out this long!

Wednesday and Thursday followed pretty much the same pattern. Magnus arrived home, had a quick shower and was off out again. She hoped his paintings never dried.

Magnus was not home when Taye went home on Friday. She got ready to go out with Julian, not looking forward to the evening in front of her one tiny bit.

Magnus was still not home when Julian came to call for her. She dragged her thoughts away from Magnus, knowing that the time had come for her to tell Julian what he had to be told. Now that the moment had arrived, though, she wanted it done now rather than at the end of the evening. But she knew she was just going to have to wait a little while. For all it would hopefully not take long to do, no way did she want Magnus to walk in in the middle of it. Julian deserved better.

'I thought we'd go somewhere a bit special tonight,' he announced enthusiastically as they drove in and out of traffic.

'I—um...' Oh, grief! How could she tell him in some place that was 'a bit special' that it was marking the last time they went out together?

She could not, Taye realised. She just could not. She could, she suppose, duck telling him, but... No. Do it now. They had just pulled up in a parking space when Taye took her courage in both hands.

Julian was just about to open the driver's door when— 'Julian!' She stopped him, and plunged straight in while she could. 'I'm afraid this will be our last meeting outside of the office.'

'What?' He was shocked and, clearly having his own agenda, had not picked up that she had been backing away this last couple of weeks. 'You can't mean that!' he exclaimed and, in shock, blurted out, 'I was going to ask you to marry me!'

It was difficult to say then who was the more stunned. 'I...' she said helplessly. 'I'm sorry. But...'

'Is it something I've said? Something I've done?'

'Oh, Julian, you've been super to go out with,' she assured him—and spent the next half-hour trying to convince him that there was no fault with him, and that it was just that, while she cared for him, it was not enough to marry him.

She was all for cancelling the rest of the evening, but Julian would not hear of that. 'If I'm not to see you again, at least let me have this one last evening with you,' he insisted.

Weakly, she agreed. But the evening was not a success. They both tried. But she found Julian's sad eyes on her so many times, and she found that much too upsetting.

But she was more upset when, having driven her home, they stood outside her apartment building and he suddenly urged, 'Marry me, Taye?' And, when numbly she shook her head, 'Do please think about it?' he asked. 'I love you enough for two of us.'

'Oh, Julian, please don't!' she whispered, and wanted to give him a gentle kiss of healing but knew that she dared not. He had appeared to misunderstand that the dates she had been on with him were just that and nothing more. The state he was in now he would misunderstand totally any final kiss in the empathy of the moment. 'I'll still see you at work,' she said gently, while wondering even then if she was going to have to consider getting a job elsewhere.

Eventually he stood back, and she went indoors. Taye felt as close to tears as she had ever been. Julian was nice, kind and good, and despite not wanting to hurt him, hurt him she had. And that hurt her.

For once as she went in she would not have minded having the apartment to herself. But there was a line of light beneath the sitting room door. And, while her heart went squishy to know that Magnus was home, she did not want to see him.

From courtesy, however, she opened the door, but did not go in. She tossed an, 'I'm home!' in through the open doorway and went on to her room.

A few seconds later, after the briefest tap on her door, she found she had company. She had her back to the door when Magnus came in. She did not turn round. 'What's wrong?' he asked.

She supposed her voice had sounded a little choked. 'Nothing,' she answered—and discovered she was looking at Magnus when he did no more than come round and stand in front of her.

'Fraser? You've been out with Fraser again!' he accused.

She bridled at his tone. 'No, I haven't!' she retorted.

'Julian Coombs?'

'You're prying again!' she snapped.

'You've been out with Julian Coombs,' Magnus decided, and, his tone softening, 'You've told him you're not going to see him again?'

Leave me alone! Taye gave a shaky sigh. She somehow knew in advance that Magnus was unlikely to leave her alone until she had answered his every question. 'I don't want to talk about it,' she said stiffly.

'Oh, poor Taye. You told him, he took it badly—and now you're hurting that you've had to cause him pain.'

'What makes you so smart?'

'It comes naturally,' Magnus teased—the back of his hand stroking down the side of her face. 'I'd love to cuddle you better, but to be honest, sweetheart, you're much too heady a woman for me to try that again.'

That shook her. She raised her head to stare at him.

Magnus thought her a heady woman? She opened her mouth, her head empty of words. Then she found a few.

'In that case, you'd better clear off,' she replied.

He looked at her long and hard, observed that she did not look quite as disquieted as she had a minute or two ago, and then said softly, 'Perhaps I had better.' And did so.

When Taye lay down in her bed shortly afterwards she began to feel guilty. Because it was not sad thoughts of Julian that kept her awake, as she might have supposed, but thoughts of Magnus. He had wanted to give her a cuddle, a kind of hug, but thought her too heady to attempt it!

She remembered how their lovemaking had begun last Sunday with Magnus giving her a cuddle. And she knew he had been right not to give in to that sensitive impulse. Because a cuddle could so easily become a kiss—and what then? Should neither of them back away from what would naturally follow—where did they go from there?

Ultimately one of them would have to leave. She faced that square on. And Taye just did not want to think of her life without Magnus in it.

CHAPTER EIGHT

IT WAS Saturday and there was no need for Taye to get up early. But already the sun was shining and she was awake and restless. She got out of bed and, remembering how the previous Saturday Magnus had remarked on her 'messed up hair', for all he had called it 'fetching', just in case he was up and about she dragged a comb through her hair before she donned her satin wrap and made for the kitchen.

There was no sign of him as she made a pot of tea and alternately thought of him and thought, sadly, of Julian. She recalled how last night Magnus had commented that he thought her a heady woman, and while just remembering that caused *her* a few heady moments, she then reflected how she had hurt Julian.

Taye poured herself a cup of tea and, feeling bad about Julian, put the cosy on the teapot and, taking her tea with her, padded to the sitting room.

While sipping her tea she mulled over what she should do that day. There were the usual chores, of course, but nothing that could not be shelved if she had a better offer.

She wondered what Magnus would be doing with his Saturday. He could be intending to work, she supposed. Being a self-employed artist wasn't the same as having a Monday-to-Friday nine-to-five occupation.

Or would he be taking his laundry to his mother? Taye was not so sure that she believed that was what he had done last Saturday—when he had come home and seen her in the bath. But she did not want to think about that!

It was true enough, though, that, while his linen was always clean, she had never seen him up to his elbows in soapsuds; she had an idea he would not know one dial on a washing machine from another.

Taye was on the point of returning her cup and saucer to the kitchen when she heard sounds that told her Magnus was on the move. He was up early too! Perhaps he was packing up his laundry to take to his mother. Jealousy struck! Perhaps he was eager to get to his lady love, Elspeth—Taye rather thought Pen-Penelope had long since had the old heave-ho.

Taye heard a nearer sound, and for no reason jumped up from her chair. Somehow she did not feel ready to see Magnus. She decided to wait until she heard the shower running and then she would slip back to her room.

It did not work out like that. For one thing Magnus did not go straight to take his shower but wandered into the sitting room, where she was. He was robe-clad—and terrific with it.

'I didn't know you were up,' he remarked casually when he saw her.

Her heart was pounding all at once, and she suddenly felt all emotional just from seeing him. She turned from him and ambled over to the window, as if finding the view from the sitting room of utmost interest. 'There's tea in the pot,' she thought to mention as she strove to get herself more of one piece.

But tea was of no concern to him just then, apparently, and she felt her heartbeats begin to pick up again when Magnus strolled over to her.

She had her gaze fixed firmly on the big old apple tree in the garden when Magnus quietly asked, 'Still feeling as upset this morning?'

He meant over Julian, of course. 'You know how it is,' she said over her shoulder.

'It upset you to have to hurt him,' Magnus sympathised. But, his tone sharpening, 'You *did* tell him you wouldn't see him again?'

'I'll have to see him at work sometimes.'

Magnus decided that was a yes. 'He took it badly?'

Taye was momentarily back with Julian. Yes, he had taken it badly. 'He asked me to marry him,' she said absently, but rapidly came to and quickly added, 'I didn't mean to tell you that!'

'Too late. I heard,' Magnus replied, and came a few steps nearer. But he was still having a mighty effect on her and she moved away—forward—which brought her that bit closer to the window. He was standing directly behind her when she felt his hands come and take a grip on her shoulders. How she did not leap a foot into the air she did not know, but she had herself outwardly under control when he demanded, 'And you said?'

'What?'

'When Coombs asked you to marry him. You said?'

Magnus's hands were burning on her shoulders through the thin satin material of her kimono. 'You know what I said,' she replied a little shakily.

There was silence for a moment before Magnus reminded her, 'You're aware that the Coombs empire is worth a mint? That he can give you everything?'

'I'm aware of that,' Taye responded. And found she was adding, 'But I don't love him.'

'You'd marry for love—not money?'

This was getting too serious. 'Don't be disgusting!' she said, with a trace of a laugh.

Magnus did not laugh, but questioned, 'You're still determined not to marry a poor man, Taye?'

She gave a small sigh. It seemed to her then that she had changed greatly since she had first known Magnus. It was no longer of importance to her whether the man she married was poor or rich, or even somewhere in between, so long as he loved her—as she loved him.

She looked out to the apple tree, saw what she had come to think of as her star, dazzling, twinkling away as the breeze turned it. And somehow found that either Magnus had taken a small step forward or she had taken a half-step back, because she was all at once leaning back against his chest.

She was so aware of him she could barely breathe. She did not want to jerk away; that would take away what for either him or her had been something sweet and natural. But something light was called for, so she pointed through the window to the apple tree.

'See that star?' She continued to point, then announced, 'I shall only marry the man who is brave enough to climb that tree and get it for me.'

With that, wanting to keep the mood light, but feeling self-conscious suddenly, she turned and discovered that Magnus still had his hands on her shoulders, and that his head was much too close to her.

Grey eyes smiled into worried blue ones and, as though to kiss away her fears, her worries, Magnus lightly touched his lips to hers. He pulled back, yet somehow seemed reluctant to let go his hold of her.

'Now see what you made me do!' he complained.

Her lips twitched. 'I get the blame for everything around here,' she complained in kind, but as he held her she found she was powerless to be the first one to make a move to break the moment.

'You know we're going to be in trouble if I do what I want to do and kiss you again?'

Taye swallowed hard. 'I somehow don't think there's been enough of that sort of trouble in my life,' she murmured huskily.

'Stop it,' he ordered. 'Behave yourself.'

She grinned up at him. 'Why should I?'

He looked down at her, down into her sparkling eyes, his glance straying to her inviting mouth, and back up to her eyes. 'Right now I can't think of one single solitary reason,' he breathed, and, gathering her into his arms, his head came down.

She felt the heat of him through her thin wrap, felt the warmth of his kiss, and was at once on fire for him as they exchanged, gave, received kiss for kiss. She was not thinking but was just one mass of loving emotion when Magnus led her to the large padded sofa. He held her close to him and they kissed and held and kissed—and held more closely.

And when Magnus moved with her she willingly lay down on the sofa with him, the ache in her heart for him for the moment quieted as he kissed her eyes, her face, his kisses straying to her throat.

'Taye,' he breathed, and she clutched on to him with no idea, as her bare feet touched the bare skin of his legs, of when she had parted with her slippers.

'Magnus.' She whispered his name, and as his hands undid her wrap, the closer to get to her, so she loosened his robe, her hands caressing his skin.

'Oh, sweetheart,' he breathed, and kissed her long and hungrily.

And she wanted more. She kissed him in return, her heart hammering as his hands caressed her breasts, a fire storming through her when he kissed her again, and once more breathed her name.

She was his, all his when, gently caressing her, those

tenderly caressing hands moved beneath her and she felt his touch on the pert globes of her buttocks, pulling her that bit closer to him.

Taye wanted to be closer to him; she felt his hard body against her and swallowed. She wanted him, oh, how she wanted him.

And yet there was a nagging something going on in her head. She felt his tongue on her lips and instinctively arched her body to him. She heard his groan of wanting and almost matched it with a moan of her own desire for him.

But that stubborn insisting annoyance in her head was thundering its way through—and Taye was struggling to sit up.

'No!' It was Magnus's voice in protest.

'Oh, Magnus!' she cried, as he too sat up.

She looked at him, and it seemed to her that he knew that the barrier she was trying to erect was only of the flimsiest. She thought he looked as though he might bring her to lie down with him again—when she knew she would be utterly and completely lost. Just one more kiss and her will to resist him would be gone.

But, manfully, when it still looked as though he would haul her back into his arms, haul her back against him, he made some space between them—and actually pushed her wrap back on to her shoulders. Though he still did not seem one hundred per cent in control when he commented, 'You're still determined to keep out of the tulip field?'

She had to smile. With her face still flushed from his lovemaking, she had to smile. 'Oh, Magnus,' she said softly, most of her defences still down. 'You must know that I want to make love with you. Only...' Her words dried. She knew she had to be careful, had to watch every word she said. But, as far as she could, she wanted to be honest with him, this man whom she loved.

'Only?' he prompted, before she was ready.

'Only—I seem to have grown a bit—er—attached to my flat-mate.'

Magnus's brow went back. Then his expression suddenly became never more serious as, sitting beside her, he looked into her eyes. 'You—have?' he asked quietly—and seemed as though he might move closer up to her.

'Don't come any nearer!' she exclaimed in panic. She was still striving to come down from that high plateau he had taken her to, and knew she would go rocketing up again if he came an inch closer. 'But if we did—you know—' She broke off, striving desperately to piece together and put into words that which was spinning around in her subconscious and wanting to take shape. 'If we did,' she picked up, 'th-then ultimately one of us would have to leave, and...' Words failed her.

But not Magnus, solemn now, intent somehow. 'And you don't want that?' he pressed.

Just then she had a feeling she would settle for anything. But deep down she knew that she wanted to be loved by Magnus, not have some brief and, to him, meaningless affair. Besides, he still had Elspeth.

Taye shook her head. 'No,' she agreed. 'I don't.' She stood up then, starting to get worried that if she said much more she would give away something of how much he truly meant to her. She rather thought she had given him some kind of a hint anyway, and she searched feverishly for some witty exit line. But all she could find to say was a rather staccato-sounding, 'As the song says—I've grown accustomed to your face.'

She looked at him, startled by her own words, and

hoped quite desperately that he would think she meant
that because she loved living there she did not want to
be the one to leave—and also that she would rather have
him as her flat-share than have to start looking for someone new all over again.

But by then Magnus was on his feet also, and was
looking at her as though he was under some kind of strain
too. And abruptly it was as though he had just come to
some kind of important decision. 'Taye,' he said, a note
of some kind of deliberation there in his voice. 'Taye,
there's something I need to tell you.'

No! She knew what that something was, and did not
want to hear it. All too plainly he had seen her love for
him, but needed to tell her that he was in love with
Elspeth—quite possibly about to get engaged to her.

'No time!' Taye said quickly, and was already halfway
to the door. 'Busy day,' she offered by way of explana-
tion. 'Better go and get dressed.' She had been a bit of
a sprinter in her school sports days; she discovered she
could still move like lightning when the occasion demanded it.

Taye showered and dressed, trying with all she had to
keep her thoughts and emotions at bay. But found to do
so totally was impossible.

She had loved being in Magnus's arms, And, next door
to being engaged to his lady-love Elspeth though he
might be, Taye felt that he had liked her responding to
him the way that she had.

She tried to hate him for that. He was a man, wasn't
he? Why wouldn't he enjoy having some young woman
clinging on to him, eager for his kisses?

But she could not hate him. Somehow, even with
Elspeth somewhere in the background, Taye could not
believe that Magnus was like that—a kiss-where-he-

could type of man. She thought of the sensitive side she had witnessed in him many times, and somehow could not believe he had taken her in his arms just because she had been there, so to speak.

When Taye got around to thinking that in that case did it not follow that Magnus must have some kind of small caring for her, she knew she needed to get away from where he was and clear her head.

Not yet ready to see him again, she waited until she heard him taking a shower and then, taking up her shoulder bag and picking up her shopping basket *en route*, she went quickly from the apartment.

She might have put some space between them physically, but Magnus was in her head the whole of the time. Taye supposed she must have been away from the apartment for an hour when her resolve to spend the morning away began to weaken. She was no nearer to clearing her head than she had been. And her emotions were still in a scaled-down traumatic uproar. But somehow something seemed to be calling her back.

She did not question what that something was. It was bound to be connected in some way with Magnus anyway. But she had to return to the home she shared with him, simply because she could stay away no longer.

Though as she let herself in she determined to keep any conversation between them on a non-personal level. And also to keep her distance from him; at least three yards' distance. Although there was something so magnetic about him three yards did not seem nearly far enough away.

Disappointment awaited her in that when she went in there was no sign of him. She dropped her shopping basket down in the kitchen and stood and listened for any sound that would tell her that Magnus was about some-where in the apartment. All was quiet.

She put her shopping away and wished she had come home sooner, while the proud part of her wished she had not come back at all. With the whole day in front of her and guessing, as her jealousy demon tormented her mer-cilessly, that he was spending *his* day with some female, Taye wandered from the kitchen into the sitting room.

She was proudly sure that she did not— Suddenly pride and all thoughts of anything else ceased, everything in her freezing in horror! For, on glancing through the sitting room window, while not being fully aware of do-ing so, a jumbled heap of clothes on the garden path suddenly took shape in her vision: a jumbled-up bundle of clothes that had not been there when she had looked out earlier. And as that clothes bundle at once started to take shape—one leg emerging, a head and an arm—so Taye was released from her momentary frozen spasm of horror and—with terror in her heart—she took off.

She reached Magnus's collapsed and crumpled-up fig-ure in no time flat, and was not thinking, just feeling, as she sank to her knees beside him.

'Magnus!' she croaked hoarsely.

He opened his eyes, looked at her, saw her concern, her panic—and who knew what else?—and suddenly he smiled. 'And for my next trick...' he began, striving to sit up.

'Don't move!' she instructed urgently, striving hard to keep a lid on her panic as blood streamed down the side of his face. Had he passed out for some reason and banged his head? Or tripped and fallen over something? she wondered worriedly. 'I'll get—'

'I'm all right.' Magnus ignored her instruction and be-gan to sit up.

'You're not supposed to move!' she admonished him. He was now bleeding profusely, she saw, her blue eyes agitatedly on his watching grey eyes.

'Love me?' Magnus asked, his eyes steady on hers.

Her heart somersaulted at his question. 'That was some bang on the head.' She sidestepped the question, her heart pounding in fear for him, for his head and a possible concussion. There was fear for herself too, and what in the stress of the moment she might unwarily let fall. 'Have you hurt yourself anywhere else?'

He shook his head—and shared some of his blood with her. 'You do love me?' he insisted.

'You're not safe let out on your own!' she complained, her emotions starting to get all tangled up again as she found her handkerchief and held it in the general direction of the source of the bloodflow.

'Then...' Magnus said, and took a deep breath before continuing, 'I think you had better marry me.' Taye froze again, and there was such a roaring in her ears just then that she could hardly believe she had heard what she thought she had just heard. Had Magnus just said what she thought he had just said? Apparently he had. Because while she was still staring at him, transfixed, although he paraphrased it, he repeated it. 'You are going to marry me, Taye, aren't you?'

He did not know what he was saying, what he was asking, she decided. That bang on his head, or whatever it was, had given him a slight concussion. But he was waiting. And, bang on the head, concussion or not, there was no way she could tell him no—particularly as, when he had got himself more of one piece, he was not going to recall any of this conversation. 'We'll—um—be poor.' She found her voice to answer him at last.

Magnus beamed the most wonderful smile at what he

saw as her acceptance of his proposal, and placed a hand over the one of hers that was holding the make-do handkerchief pad to his head. He looked quite delighted. 'We'll have babies,' he informed her.

'That'll be fun!' she retorted, thinking that maybe she should nip this kind of talk in the bud right now.

'Won't it, though?' Magnus answered wickedly—and suddenly they were both grinning idiotically.

But Taye, the one looking at the blood still streaming down his face, was the first to recover. 'We'd better see about getting you to hospital,' she said firmly.

'No chance,' he replied—and there was that in his tone that clearly told her she would be wasting her breath in arguing.

'Well, at least let me get you inside so I can inspect the damage!' she exclaimed shortly, and felt relief when he allowed her to help him to his feet.

She was not sure it was strictly necessary for him to place an arm about her shoulders as they went up the path, but she could not deny she liked his arm there. And, just in case he needed her as a prop, she put an arm around his waist.

'Kitchen,' she said as they went into the house. 'Sit here,' she suggested and, when he meekly complied, she went in search of a scrappy sort of first-aid box, hoping there was everything there that she would need. 'I'll try not to hurt you,' she said kindly when she returned.

'I'm sure you have the touch of an angel,' Magnus replied politely—and did not so much as murmur as Taye got busy with water and cotton wool and began to clean away the blood.

'Good heavens!' she exclaimed, when she eventually got to the source of the problem—the smallest cut, about an inch above his left eyebrow.

'Am I going to live?' he teased.

'All that blood, and it's only the tiniest nick!'

'You're not going to have to sew it up for me, then?'

She smiled, wanting to hug him, wanting to kiss him, and just to hold him he was so dear to her. 'I think, in my professional opinion, you'll get by without it needing a stitch. Though until it stops bleeding you're going to have to wear a plaster.'

'Anything you say, Nurse,' he replied—now that she had lifted the threat of a hospital visit ready to agree to anything she said, it seemed.

Taye loved the intimacy of the moment as, close up to him, she put a small adhesive dressing on his wound. She had to make quite an effort to stand back from him. 'I think you may want to change your shirt,' she commented of his blood-soaked shirt.

Magnus got to his feet, his eyes gentle on her. 'I've bloodied your shirt too,' he said apologetically.

'Not a problem!' she murmured, stepping further back to give him some space.

She thought he would go straight away, but he delayed to quietly ask, 'You won't try to avoid me again?'

She stared at him. From that she gathered that he knew she had been out, perhaps knew too that, all het-up from their lovemaking, she had not then been yet ready to face him. 'I'd better go and change too!' she said in a hurry, and was halfway to the door when his voice reached her.

'Got a kiss for your fiancé?' he asked.

Stunned, she halted. Then turned. His expression was serious, stern almost, as she tried to read his eyes. Her heart was pounding away so furiously she felt she could hardly breathe. 'I… You…' she gasped. And, whether he thought she was avoiding him or whether he didn't, it was just then all too much for her.

Her emotions had been on the jangle all morning. And that had been before he had kissed her and she had kissed him. She had bolted—ostensibly to shop—and had returned half fearing she had found him dead. And now this! It was all too much. Much too much! Taye turned about again—and fled.

CHAPTER NINE

TAYE made it to her bedroom door and raced in, hurriedly closing the door behind her. Magnus could not be serious, could he? Agitatedly she collapsed on to a chair, could not sit still, and got up again. He had looked serious, though, she recalled, her mouth dry.

Yes, but he had just received a bang to his head, argued that piece of her she would much prefer not to listen to. She recalled all the blood on his clothes, albeit that the wound was such a small one.

No, he could not have been serious, argued her saner self. Somehow or other he'd had an accident, collapsed dazed and confused on the garden path, and had still been dazed and confused when she had found him.

There was every likelihood, Taye decided, that once he had recovered—most probably any time now— Magnus would remember nothing of what had taken place in the garden or, for that matter, the kitchen.

She had just begun to wonder if she should go back and check that he was all right, when she heard sounds of him moving around. Her fears for him momentarily abated, she then heard the shower running.

Taye listened, fear rising again in case, still not quite himself, Magnus might slip in the shower while rinsing the blood off. But he was safe. A few minutes later the plumbing noises stopped, and a few minutes after that she heard him leave the bathroom.

She looked down at her own blood-splattered self and

considered a quick shower would be the easiest way of cleaning herself up.

Fifteen minutes later, dressed in a fresh tee shirt and jeans, Taye was in her room wondering what to do for the best. She knew she would have to face Magnus some time, and she wanted to see him—of course she did. But the more she thought about it, the more she began to believe that he must have seen her love for him. But it would be just too utterly humiliating should he refer to it, yet feel nothing for her himself.

Yet would he do that? He was far more sensitive than she had at first given him credit for. And anyway, hadn't she already judged that he would most likely not remember any of what had taken place either in the garden or in the kitchen?

That last thought, spurred on by her need to see him and get this over with, saw Taye leaving her bedroom. Still the same she hesitated at the sitting room door, and had to take a moment to get herself a little together before she went in.

Magnus was there, as she'd hoped—not hoped. He was standing with his eyes on the door, clearly waiting for her. She felt her colour rising and hated that tell-tale blush that gave away that just seeing him again affected her emotionally.

She decided to get in first. 'How's the head?' she asked, her eyes on the strip of plaster above his left eye, her words sounding uneven and jittery even to her own ears. Feeling still too strung up to be able to sit down, she went to stand at the back of an armchair.

Magnus studied her, seeming calm where she was all over the place. 'No kiss yet?' he enquired politely.

He might have been trying to relieve her tension, might have been trying to make her smile, but what he had done was to remind her—and she had not forgotten—that his last words to her had been, 'Got a kiss for your fiancé?'

'I—um—wasn't sure you knew what you were saying,' she responded cautiously. 'I—thought perhaps you wouldn't remember any of what happened—er—in the garden.'

'I remember everything,' Magnus replied steadily. And, his eyes watching her face, he added deliberately, 'And that includes falling out of the apple tree and—'

'You fell out of the apple tree?' she gasped, her eyes huge in her astonishment. 'What on earth were you doing...?' Her voice faded. 'You—didn't?' she questioned huskily, trying to deny what her brain was endeavouring to tell her.

'I had to,' Magnus took up, when she had no more to say but just stared at him speechlessly. 'It was only this morning that you stated, quite categorically, that you would only marry the man brave enough to climb that tree for that star.' Taye was still staring at him openmouthed when he added, 'I wasn't leaving it there for some other man to collect for you.'

'You—climbed the tree for it? For m-me?' she stammered, her head in a whirl.

'For you,' he confirmed, and, dipping his hand into his trouser pocket, he withdrew the star that for the last seven or so months had rested, snagged, in the old apple tree. 'So you see, Taye, my very dear Taye,' he said quietly, coming over and handing the star to her, 'that even without your earlier acceptance of my proposal, you are in receipt of that token which makes you honourbound to marry me.' Her heart was thundering. She wanted to speak—but was powerless to find her voice. 'You'd agree, I hope?' Magnus insisted.

He was serious. He *was* serious! 'It would seem I have

very little choice—but to agree,' she answered, with what breath she could find.

'Sweet darling,' Magnus murmured tenderly, and at his tone, never mind the spine-melting endearment, her legs went to water. He made to come nearer, but Taye was in such a state of wanting to believe she had just agreed to marry him, and in such a state of not believing he could have asked her to marry him, that she took a step back. And he halted, his expression questioning.

'You—um—care about me a little—then?' Taye found she just had to ask. She needed to know. Oh, how she needed to know.

'Oh, I care about you, Taye Trafford,' he assured her. 'You, and thoughts of you, have filled my head since that first day I met you.'

'Oh!' she sighed, and was ready to melt completely— until ice-cold reasoning plugged in, switched on, and gave her a jolt. 'From day one?' she questioned—would she ever forget the surly brute he had been when they had first met?

'From day one,' Magnus confirmed, his eyes fixed on hers, the cooling of her tone not lost on him. 'I wouldn't lie to you over a thing like that.'

Taye stared at him, her mind in something of a major turmoil. 'Are you intimating that you have lied about other things?' she asked.

And Magnus expelled a sharp breath. 'One of the things that attracted me to you, and there are many, is your quick intelligence,' he said after a moment, and while Taye's heart raced to hear that many things about her attracted him he went on, 'So I suppose I can hardly complain that you're not going to meet me at the altar without me first giving you the answers to some of the questions that are likely to crop up.'

Taye watched him, and wanted quite desperately then to be held and kissed by him. But it sounded to her very much as if he was admitting that he had lied to her—and that was no basis for a marriage, was it?

'You lied to me?' she queried, finding, even though she was still wilting at the thought of meeting him at the altar, that she could not let it go. There had been lies in her parents' marriage—there would be no room for them in hers.

'I've tried not to,' Magnus answered carefully.

'But you have?'

He nodded. 'I've avoided having to lie wherever possible, but, the situation being what it was, I'm afraid there have been times when to lie has been unavoidable.'

Situation? What situation? Taye stared at him totally uncomprehending. 'You're the one with the bang on the head, right? So why do I feel as if I'm the one who's disorientated? I'm sorry, Magnus, but I cannot see any logical reason why you should lie to me.' She strove hard to see, but still could not. 'I mean, I know you're an artist and probably see things a little differently, perhaps. But—'

'I'm not an artist,' he cut in quietly. 'I want to be completely honest with you now, T—'

'You're *not* an artist?' she butted in, feeling winded. 'But—but you asked me to pose for you—in the nude!' she exclaimed, vividly remembering how that had come about. She had been naked in the bath...

'Oh, I knew in advance you'd say no,' Magnus interrupted, to save her further blushes.

Her amazement seemed to increase with every word he uttered. 'So, you're not an artist,' she itemised when she came up for air.

'I had to tell you something,' he owned up. 'And you'd

spotted paint on one of my fingers. To be an artist was the first thing that came to mind.'

She was still having difficulty taking this in. 'But you're not—yet you had to tell me something?' She looked at him sharply. 'So what is it you do do—if you don't mind me asking? You're not a bank robber or anything shady like that?'

'Nothing at all like that,' he reassured her. 'The opposite, if anything.' But, before going on, 'Look, Taye, I realise I have a lot to tell you, a lot of explaining to do,' he said. 'It—humph—could take a little while. Shall we sit down over there?' he said, indicating the sofa where only that morning they had lain together.

Taye was unsure. She somehow felt a need to keep her head, but, remembering Magnus's kisses, the kiss he was still waiting for from his fiancée—oh, heavens, fiancée—how was she to keep her head if he kissed her again? Aside from anything else, she did not know when, if ever, she would come down to earth again had his proposal that she marry him been for real. Yet, crazily, she somehow found she had started to believe that it had been for real. 'I don't know…' she demurred, even as she wanted to hear everything he had to say. But, looking over to the sofa, 'You won't try any of that—kissing stuff…?' His sudden smile made her break off. She guessed he knew what the kisses they shared did to her.

Magnus held out his hand. 'I promise I'll hold off from kissing you for as long as I'm able,' he agreed.

Taye was not very sure what sort of security she should read into that kind of a promise, but she loved the man and, after a moment, moved from behind the armchair and let him take her hand in his and lead her over to the sofa.

She quickly retrieved her hand once they were seated,

however, and began to think it about time she started
asking a few questions. She had no idea what Magnus
had meant by 'the situation being what it was' but, first
things first, she thought she would like to know why he
had lied about being an artist.

'So,' she turned to him to enquire, 'what sort of job
do you do that is the opposite of robbing banks?'

'I endeavour to make them burglarproof,' he promptly
answered. 'I run a company that specialises in high tech
security systems for the home and overseas commercial
sector.'

'You run it!' Taye exclaimed.

'Somebody has to,' he answered modestly.

And suddenly then the fact that his clothes looked expensive all at once took on a new meaning. 'I thought
you were broke!' she said, wide-eyed. 'But you're not,
are you?'

'Not,' he agreed.

'You're—quite—um—well-to-do?' she pressed.

'Quite,' he replied, watching her as she took in the
information that the man she'd believed struggled as she
did to find the rent was in actual fact quite financially
sound, and then some, thank you very much.

Taye looked at him, not feeling in the least amused.
'Then would you mind very much telling me exactly
what you are doing living here in rented accommodation?'

'A question I have frequently asked myself,' Magnus
replied, which to her mind was no sort of an answer.

'And would I be right in assuming that not only can
you very easily afford to pay the quarterly rent, but that
you could probably afford to buy this flat if it came up
for sale?'

'And the rest of the building,' Magnus informed her pleasantly.

Taye closed her mouth, barely knowing when it had fallen open in shock. To be able to buy the whole of the building would make him some kind of millionaire!

She swallowed. 'You're joking, right?'

'Not joking,' he replied seriously, and stayed serious to ask quickly, 'You're still going to marry me?'

Her heart gave one of its giddy leaps, and she tried desperately to keep her feet planted firmly on the ground. 'I think it's high time, Mr Ashthorpe...' Her voice tailed off, something in his expression, that silent Oh his wonderful mouth formed, alerting her to perhaps another lie. 'What?' she asked.

'Hmm—Ashthorpe is my middle name,' Magnus replied.

'Ashthorpe is—' She broke off, stupefied. 'You're not Magnus Ash... Mr Ashthorpe?'

'I'm afraid not.'

Taye took a shaky breath. 'Then I suggest, Mr Who-ever-you-are...that you start talking,' she told him severely. She would much prefer that he took her in his arms. But it seemed to her—and confused wasn't the word for how she felt—that a lot had been going on here. And if they were to have any sort of a life together—her heart raced again at how wonderful that sounded—then that could only happen, for her anyway, from an open and truthful basis. And, by his own admission, Magnus had not shirked from lying to her.

Magnus looked at her, stretched out a hand and tenderly stroked a strand of white-blonde hair back from her face, and, while her heart did a giddy flip again at his tender gesture, 'I came here that first day...'

'Nick-Mick Knight didn't ask you to leave his flat, did he?' she butted in.

'He did not.'

'His girlfriend wasn't moving in with him?'

'I don't know that she exists.'

'You invented her?' Magnus nodded. 'And him?' Taye asked, and, sensing she was right, 'Is there any such person as Nick Knight?'

'Most likely. Though I've never come across him,' he admitted.

Taye looked at Magnus, her brain racing in competition with her heartbeats. 'So—if you weren't living at Nick Knight's address prior to moving in here, where were you living?'

'I have my own place,' Magnus replied, ready to at once answer her every question, it seemed.

'Then why…?'

'Why move in here?' Magnus took her next question. 'Well, for one—and for several—other matters had arrived to take precedence over the extended holiday I'd planned to take while my house was being redecorated throughout.'

Taye saw what he meant by for one—and for several. By the sound of it Magnus had a house and had booked decorators to do his place up while he went on holiday. Only something else had happened, arrived, to make him cancel his holiday. And, since he had probably waited some while to get a good firm of decorators to give him a start date, he had decided not to cancel the decorators.

'You decided, rather than put the decorators off, that you would rent for a short while?' Taye enquired, and, bridling suddenly, 'And you had the nerve to get umpty with me when I told you I would have to find somewhere smaller, cheaper to live, when you had no intention of staying yourse—'

'I had every intention then, as now, of continuing to live with you, and still do,' Magnus broke in, well and truly taking the wind from her sails.

'Oh,' she murmured, feeling just a tinge pink, though with the way her heart was misbehaving not at all surprised. 'You—um—didn't fancy going to a hotel while the decorators were in? Or to your mother's? Or—' as that demon green-eyed monster nipped '—your friend Elspeth?' Taye asked.

Magnus smiled, quite liking her shade of green, it seemed, though his expression was serious when, like balm over a deep wound, he informed her, 'Elspeth, is my sister.' His sister! 'She is going through an extremely difficult time right now.'

'Oh, I'm so sorry!' Taye was instantly apologetic. But, not wanting to pry into what was clearly a family matter, and particularly not wanting to say a word about Elspeth that would indicate how many times jealousy had swamped her, Taye went in another direction, 'So you saw the card advertising half a flat to let here, and—' Magnus shaking his head caused her to break off.

'I didn't see that card until after I'd left here that Saturday,' he said.

'You—didn't?' Bewildered wasn't the word for it! 'But how did you know there was a flat-share available?'

'I didn't know. In fact it wasn't until I had let myself in through the main door and, just in case the present occupant was in some state of *déshabillé,* had knocked on the door instead of coming straight in, that—'

'Just a minute!' she interrupted him quickly. 'Are you saying that you had a set of keys *before* I gave you a set?'

Magnus smiled at her. 'Are you sure you wouldn't like me to kiss you?' he asked.

Oh, stop it, stop it, stop it! Didn't he know how pathetically weak she was where he was concerned? 'I'm sure,' she lied—lying wasn't his sole prerogative. 'You already had a set of keys.' She managed to remember what they had been talking about. 'How?' she asked. 'Did Paula give them to you? I didn't think you knew her? You—'

'I don't know her,' he replied. And, solemnly then, he said, 'But I know her man-friend.'

Taye looked questioningly at him. 'You know Graeme?'

'He was married to Elspeth,' Magnus informed her quietly.

'He—he was married to your sister?' Startled to hear that, Taye thought for a moment. 'That would be before they divorced and he started going out with Paula?' It was the only thing that seemed to fit.

'My sister and Graeme Lockwood were never divorced,' Magnus revealed. 'Graeme was still married, and living with Elspeth, at the same time he was having an affair with Paula Neale.'

Taye was dumbstruck. 'They were still together while…?'

'Happily together, as far as Elspeth was concerned.'

'She had no idea that he…?' Words failed her.

'Not the smallest idea. She still doesn't know,' Magnus said. 'I intend to keep it that way.'

'You don't think Graeme will confess at—'

'Graeme's dead,' Magnus bluntly stated. And, at Taye's look of shock, for all she had never met his brother-in-law, 'He was killed in a motor accident,' Magnus said. 'He worked for me and—'

'He worked for you?' Taye exclaimed. Then something suddenly clicked in her brain and she was glad to
find that the memory part of her brain was not as totally
stupefied as she herself felt. 'Hadn't Graeme worked for
a security equipment company? At Penhaligon's?' she
questioned. Penhaligon's was a massive firm, so that part
of it did not take too much memory retrieval to recall.
But then something else struck her and she took a deep
if shaky breath. 'If you're not Ashthorpe—well, you are,
in the middle, but—pardon me if I sound muddled; I
thought I was confused before but...' She swallowed.
'Tell me you're not Penhaligon at the end?'

Magnus looked a shade uncomfortable, she thought,
but manfully owned, 'I am,' and while she stared at him
dumbfounded he found a gentle smile for her and nicely
offered, 'But I can change it if you don't fancy the name
Mrs Penhaligon.'

'Stop!' Taye implored him. 'I feel in one totally bewildered maze from what you've told me so far without
having to cope with the fact that you must be some kind
of multimillionaire—who could eat at Claridges every
day if you wished, and lodge at the finest of hotels, yet
have chosen to live in this abode—' She broke off, not
certain she wanted him to know how the fact he seemed
to want to make her Mrs Penhaligon was affecting her.
'C-can we please concentrate on just one particular is-
sue?' she asked shakily.

'Sweet love, anything you say,' Magnus answered, his
eyes tender on her all-at-sea expression.

'You said Graeme worked for you.' She plucked that
out from a head racing with But whys.

'He did,' Magnus took up. 'He was good at his job
too. Elspeth at one time worked for the firm also. It was
how they met. And though she still popped in to the firm

from time to time, she thought it politic to resign when they married. But when Graeme died she was absolutely distraught—so distraught, in fact, that when she found what was obviously a desk drawer key amongst his belongings she just could not face going to his office to pick up his personal effects.'

'I can understand that,' Taye put in quietly, and received a warm smile from the man sitting next to her.

'I insisted that she didn't have to, that I would do it.'

'It was how you found out that he was having an affair?' she guessed. 'A letter or something…'

'A lease to this apartment, actually,' Magnus corrected her. 'And with it a set of keys.'

'A—lease? Paula's lease?' Taye stated that which her startled intelligence had brought her.

'The lease was in Graeme's name.'

'Oh!' Taye exclaimed, but after a moment or two recovered to ask, 'You began to suspect…?'

'For sure I didn't want to tell Elspeth what I had found until I'd made damned sure she knew nothing of it. She was and still is having difficulty in coming to terms with the fact her dear love will not be coming home any more. It would devastate her should she learn, as I began to realise, that he had some little love-nest tucked away somewhere.'

'The mud is starting to become a little clearer,' Taye murmured. 'You decided to come and investigate?'

'Too true! I was not,' he thought to mention, 'feeling at my sunniest that morning we met.'

'Funnily enough, I did notice.'

'I didn't know then that you weren't the one Graeme had been carrying on with. Are you sure I can't kiss you?'

Her heart fluttered. 'You were saying?'

'I shall make up for it later,' he threatened. 'Please. So there was I,' he resumed, 'without the first idea of Graeme's mistress's name, knocking on the door ready to tell whoever answered that I'd been to the agents, taken over the lease pro tem, and was throwing her out.'

'You've taken over the lease?' Taye gasped, open mouthed. 'But I—but all that—about me being a sub-let—about you… And all the time…'

'I know,' he acknowledged gently. 'I didn't want any comeback on Elspeth, so needed the matter dealt with properly. Which meant I gave the agents a quarter's notice to terminate the tenancy and paid the coming quarter's rent. But I couldn't tell you any of that. Not then. And later, well…' Magnus left it there and went speedily on. 'Anyhow, there was I, incensed on my sister's behalf, and more than ready to sort out the trollop who answered the door.' Trollop! 'Then, to thoroughly deflate me, this beautiful woman with the most gorgeous blue eyes opens the door…'

'Me?' Taye asked faintly, on the instant ready to forgive him the 'trollop' remark.

'You, my darling,' Magnus replied.

'Oh,' she sighed. But, remembering how it had been, 'You didn't look as if you thought me—um—beautiful,' she reminded him.

'I was having to cope with several matters all at once,' he explained. '"You've come about the flat," you said. Well, I rather supposed I had. But by then I'm trying to ignore how taken I am by your beauty, and endeavouring to get to grips with the fact that no sooner is your provider dead than his money-grubbing lover is trying to rent out half of the flat.'

'You thought…?'

'Forget what I thought then—I soon discovered that you were as beautiful inside as you were on the outside.'

Taye drew a sharp breath. 'Carry on like that Mr Ash...Penhaligon, and I shall start to melt,' she murmured, and, regardless, was tenderly kissed.

'Sorry,' he apologised, not looking at all sorry. 'I just had to do that. So...' he continued. 'Um...' he went on, as if trying to remember. 'There was I, more interested in saving Elspeth from hurting any more than she was already hurting, while knowing that I can throw this Taye Trafford out any time I choose.'

'Too kind,' Taye murmured, but said it with a smile— and risked being on the receiving end of another kiss.

Magnus managed to hold down the impulse, however, the sooner to get it all said. 'Before I did that, though, I first of all needed to discover if this woman had any power to make problems for my sister. Elspeth was particularly fragile just then. I, my love, was without anywhere to comfortably lay my head. I particularly wanted to keep out of my mother's way, and to go to a hotel had no appeal; although I did find myself using that option several times when I needed to put some space between you and me and—'

'That weekend? Those nights away? They were...?'

'On account of you, Miss Trafford. You,' he said softly, 'were getting to me big-time.'

'Good heavens,' she whispered huskily, and had to fight hard against the almost overwhelming urge to return his compliment and tenderly kiss him. 'So?' she found a moment of restraint to question instead.

'So it seemed to me that since, with the decorators in, I had no home to go to, I might as well stay and be your sub-tenant when, by living in the same dwelling, I'd be well placed to find out more about you and what more trouble and grief, if any, you were likely to cause for Elspeth. You wanted references—as soon as I hit the pavement I was on the phone to my mother, asking her, should you ring, to give me a splendid reference.'

'That lady—um—Mrs Sturgess—is your mother? The lady I spoke with, who said she had been at school with your mother, *was* your mother?' Was there no end to the shocks she was receiving? Taye wondered.

'She's incorrigible—a dear, and a woman who loves a bit of intrigue.'

'Is that why you wanted to keep out of her way?'

'Precisely. Graeme was killed the day before I was scheduled to fly to the Bahamas. I cancelled my holiday to be there for Elspeth and subsequently sort out the muddle of his affairs—no pun intended. My mother knew my place was awash with decorators, so I hoped she'd believe I was renting some place meanwhile, and under the name of Ashthorpe because I wanted to keep a low profile.'

'Your mother swallowed that?'

'Not the Ashthorpe bit; but I knew she would back me to the hilt. Though, knowing her mammoth curiosity to get to the root of everything, I had to limit our communications to the telephone—she would have been extremely upset on Elspeth's behalf had I told her the truth. But in any event she has been fairly preoccupied in supporting Elspeth as much as she can.'

'Of course,' Taye sympathised, but, after a moment or two, 'So you moved in here…?'

'Not before I'd walked around and found a newsagent with a card in his window advertising half this flat for rent.'

'You stole that card,' she documented.

'Quite easily done,' he owned, totally unblinking.

'And, yes, I moved in—and promptly had all my theories about Graeme Lockwood's mistress go sailing out the window.'

'You discovered I—'

'Before I moved in I discovered you were nowhere near as money-grubbing as I assumed. I knew by then that the rent to the start of the June quarter had been paid by Graeme. Yet when you could have asked me for two weeks' rent up to then, you didn't. Another surprise was the fact that the quarter's rent you asked for was a straight split down the middle. And, if that wasn't enough to have me rethinking my prior opinions of you, there was your sensitivity when you obviously felt awkward about prying into my relationships.'

'You were still being a—a grouch, though,' she reminded him.

'Why wouldn't I be? Elspeth was heartbroken, but you were so un-grief-stricken that you were soon dating someone else.'

'Julian?'

'The same,' he agreed. 'It soon became very clear that you must have been two-timing Graeme. So there am I, trying to learn as much as I can about you, trying to gauge what sort of a threat you represent to my sister's already fractured peace of mind—while at the same time I'm starting to be at war with myself in that I find I'm struggling not to like you.'

'You liked me—early on?' she fished, loving him so much, wanting to know his every thought, his every emotion.

'How could I help it?' he asked simply. 'In between going to check how the decorators are doing, looking in on the office, and keeping in contact with Elspeth, I find I'm not caring very much for you dating your pal Julian

Coombs. Is it any wonder I had to take myself off to a hotel to sort myself out?'

Her eyes were big and shining as she quietly asked, 'Did you really take your washing to your mother last Saturday?'

'She'd have told me what to do with it if I had,' he said with a smile. 'Though in actual fact it was my original intention to stay away for the weekend. Only...'

'Only?' Taye prompted when he seemed hesitant to continue.

'Only I found I couldn't settle and that nothing would do but that I check out of that hotel and come home.'

'Home?'

'Home—to you,' he answered. 'Crazy, I know. Even though I was sure you wouldn't be here—you had mentioned some party invitation—I just had to come back to you.' He paused then, and, looking levelly at her, stated, 'On Sunday morning I knew exactly why.'

Taye's heart began thundering in her chest at his look; she sensed that something pretty staggering was coming. 'Sunday morning?' she asked, her voice barely above a whisper.

'I said I'd take you out to lunch,' he reminded her. 'And you bounced my invitation back at me.'

'You'll make me blush. I thought then that you couldn't afford it.'

'Sweet darling,' he said softly. 'That was when it happened,' he murmured, his eyes adoring on her face.

'What—happened?' she asked chokily, her bones turning to liquid just from his look.

'You being you. You, when I knew full well that you were as broke as makes no difference, refusing my offer but saying you would take me for a pie and a pint. Sweet love, I knew then what it was that had been battering away at the brick wall I had tried to erect from our very first meeting.' He looked deeply, tenderly into her eyes, and softly he told her, 'My darling Taye, I knew then, accepted then, that I was in love with you with my whole heart.'

'Magnus!' There was a roaring in her ears as his name left her on a breath of sound.

'That's all right with you?' he asked.

Taye found her voice. 'More than all right,' she whispered.

He smiled, seeming relieved. 'And you? How do you feel about me?'

'I knew on Sunday too,' she answered shyly.

'What?' He seemed tense all at once.

'Last Sunday, when you borrowed a car—' She broke off. '*Did* you borrow that car?' she asked.

He shook his head. 'It belongs to me,' he admitted. 'Go on,' he urged, more interested in how she felt about him than the ownership of the vehicle. 'Last Sunday?' he prompted.

'Last Sunday,' she dutifully took up, 'you were so good, so kind, and I just knew, when I came to you in the garden of my mother's home, what all the jealousy and the mixture of other emotions that have bombarded me over you were all about. I,' she said softly, 'just loved and loved you.'

'Oh, Taye!' he breathed, and, whether all his lies had been explained or whether they had not, he just had to haul her joyously into his arms and hold her. 'Dear love, you're sure?' he asked.

'It's just there. For real. I can't help it. I just love you—am in love with you—and...'

'And you can't begin to know how relieved it makes

me to hear you say that. Sweetheart…' he murmured, and all was silent for long minutes as he just had to kiss her.

And Taye just had to kiss him back, and for uncounted minutes they kissed and held each other, Magnus pulling back from time to time to look into her face, to feast his eyes on the love he saw there.

'One way and another that was one very memorable Sunday,' he said after some while.

'As it happens,' she said on a sigh, 'everything has turned out wonderfully. For us, and for Hadleigh.'

'It would have been fine for Hadleigh without your father coming to the rescue,' Magnus commented, as if it was by the way. But, at her enquiring look, 'I couldn't tell you my plan before I had confessed all my lies to you, my darling, but my idea was to financially back Hadleigh through university and—'

'He wouldn't have taken your money,' Taye interrupted. 'He's proud and…'

'I know that,' Magnus said with a smile. 'Which is why I thought I'd make a binding agreement with him that in return for Penhaligon's sponsoring him he, at the end of his studies, would enter our graduate scheme and work for a two-year term at Penhaligon Security.'

Taye stared at him in love and amazement. 'You planned…? You had this up your sleeve the whole…?'

'I couldn't tell Hadleigh then. But I knew I would have to tell you everything before too long; then I could tell your brother…'

'You were going to tell me soon?'

'Dammit, woman, I'm in love with you,' Magnus growled. 'It *had* to be soon. I couldn't hold off much longer. I want to marry you. I *need* to marry you. It's got so bad just lately,' he confessed, 'that I haven't trusted myself in the same room with you. I've sometimes had to go out, make myself stay away from here, for fear I might give in and take you in my arms.'

'Oh, Magnus. Honestly?'

'The truth only from now on, my love.'

'Only the truth from now on,' she agreed, her heart still having a high old time within her. 'Er—why…?' she began, but just had to kiss him, and be kissed for her trouble.

'Why…?' Magnus was marginally the first to recover.

'Why—um—when I told you it was Paula who had been Graeme's girlfriend, when you knew it wasn't me that might hurt Elspeth, why did you stay on here? I mean, I can appreciate with you not knowing me all that well that you wouldn't want to confide about your sister and everything, but you continued to live here—to let me live here.'

Magnus cupped the side of her face with one hand and revealed, 'While I may have realised that I'd moved in for nothing, I still didn't have anywhere else I wanted to be.' He gave a self-deprecating shrug. 'Of course I told myself that I might as well live here as anywhere until the decorators had finished. But…'

'But?'

'But the plain truth is it began to feel right coming home to you. It began to feel right being here when you came home.' He gave that self-deprecating shrug again as he confessed, 'Then I kissed you—and while every scrap of common sense was telling me to pack up and leave, right then, I was somehow finding that love—what I now know is love—and common sense just don't mix.'

Taye smiled, her smile becoming a beam—and Magnus looked at her and, his heart full of love for her, he groaned and just had to gather her to him and hold her close.

'Love me?' he asked.

'You know I do.'

'So say it,' he growled.

And, while it amazed her that a man as confident as he should need reassurance that she loved him, 'I love you, love you, love you,' she lovingly obliged. Then asked, 'Who was Penny?'

'Penny?' He pulled back, a touch mystified.

'You answered the phone—that day I rang your mobile. It had been engaged the first time I tried. So I realised when you answered the phone with her name that you must have just been speaking to her and thought she had rung back. You said "Pen and—"' She broke off at his grin.

'Pen,' he said, 'is short for Penhaligon. I instinctively went to answer the phone "Penhaligon" but, having been waiting for your call, nearly blew my whole plot.' He did not have to say any more.

'Well, I shan't have to be jealous of her any more,' Taye commented.

'Fair's only fair,' he countered. 'I was not at all happy whenever I thought of you and Coombs together—only to get eaten alive by that green stuff when you take up with Fraser!'

'I only went out with him because you accused me of being jealous.'

'Little love,' he breathed, and held her close up against him for long, long, comforting, loving seconds.

Being in his arms was utter bliss; being held by him sublime. 'There was a letter for an M. A. Penhaligon,' she murmured dreamily.

'Blundering agents,' he muttered. 'I gave specific instructions not to send any communications to me here, but to use my office address. And what do they do when they decide to send a receipt for the cheque I gave them…?'

'My cheque?'

He shook his head. 'The quarter's rent was already paid by then. I'm keeping your cheque as a souvenir. Everybody was trying to blow my cover,' he informed her lightly.

She pulled back to look at him. 'They were—' She broke off. 'Damien Fraser thought he knew you from somewhere!' she exclaimed.

'As did your father. I can only assume they both must take the financial newspapers. There's a photo of me they trot out whenever anything newsworthy in the financial area crops up—as happened recently. As luck would have it neither your father nor Fraser associated Magnus Ashthorpe with Magnus Penhaligon.'

'Beware your sins will find you out,' she teased him. 'That's what you risk when you start telling lies.'

'I'll never lie to you again,' Magnus uttered, a sincerity there that melted her heart.

'Love me?' she asked, finding, as he had, that, trust him though she did, she still needed to hear him say it.

'So much,' he responded. 'I love you so much nothing else matters but that you are in my life.'

'Oh, Magnus,' she sighed, and kissed him, and was kissed in return. Her face was a tinge pink as they pulled back and looked into each other's eyes. 'This morning, and before, when to kiss and—make love with you seemed so right,' she began shyly, 'I needed to hear you say you loved me, that it wasn't just some meaningless affair that would end with one of us leaving.'

'Oh, my dearest darling,' he breathed. 'I loved you then and I love you now. And we'll leave together.'

'We—will?' she asked huskily.

'I want you with me always,' he told her tenderly. 'I've a home just waiting for you. Please say you'll come and be my house-mate—my wife?'

'You truly want to marry me?' she whispered.

'I'll settle for nothing less,' Magnus replied, his eyes never leaving her face. 'Please, my beautiful Taye, let me hear you say you will.'

Taye smiled at him, her heart full to bursting. 'Oh, Magnus. I will. I love you so, I can't think of anything or anyone I'd rather be than Mrs Magnus Ashthorpe—Penhaligon.'

'Darling!' he cried triumphantly, and gathered her close up to him once more.

MILLS & BOON®

Live the emotion

OCTOBER 2005 HARDBACK TITLES

ROMANCE™

Blackmailing the Society Bride *Penny Jordan*
H6260 0 263 18755 1
Baby of Shame *Julia James* H6261 0 263 18756 X
Taken by the Highest Bidder *Jane Porter* H6262 0 263 18757 8
Virgin for Sale *Susan Stephens* H6263 0 263 18758 6
The Italian's Convenient Wife *Catherine Spencer*
H6264 0 263 18759 4
The Antonakos Marriage *Kate Walker* H6265 0 263 18760 8
Mistress to a Rich Man *Kathryn Ross* H6266 0 263 18761 6
Tamed by her Husband *Elizabeth Power* H6267 0 263 18762 4
A Most Suitable Wife *Jessica Steele* H6268 0 263 18763 2
In the Arms of the Sheikh *Sophie Weston* H6269 0 263 18764 0
The Marriage Miracle *Liz Fielding* H6270 0 263 18765 9
Ordinary Girl, Society Groom *Natasha Oakley*
H6271 0 263 18766 7
Christmas Due Date *Moyra Tarling* H6272 0 263 18767 5
The Billionaire's Wedding Masquerade *Melissa McClone*
H6273 0 263 18768 3
The Life Saver *Lilian Darcy* H6274 0 263 18769 1
The Noble Doctor *Gill Sanderson* H6275 0 263 18770 5

HISTORICAL ROMANCE™

The Outrageous Debutante *Anne O'Brien* H612 0 263 18821 3
The Captain's Lady *Margaret McPhee* H613 0 263 18822 1
Winter Woman *Jenna Kernan* H614 0 263 18950 3

MEDICAL ROMANCE™

Gift of a Family *Sarah Morgan* M527 0 263 18845 0
Christmas on the Children's Ward *Carol Marinelli*
M528 0 263 18846 9

MILLS & BOON®

Live the emotion

OCTOBER 2005 LARGE PRINT TITLES

ROMANCE™

Married by Arrangement *Lynne Graham*	1807	0 263 18587 7
Pregnancy of Revenge *Jacqueline Baird*	1808	0 263 18588 5
In the Millionaire's Possession *Sara Craven*		
	1809	0 263 18589 3
The One-Night Wife *Sandra Marton*	1810	0 263 18590 7
The Italian's Rightful Bride *Lucy Gordon*	1811	0 263 18591 5
Husband by Request *Rebecca Winters*	1812	0 263 18592 3
Contract To Marry *Nicola Marsh*	1813	0 263 18593 1
The Mirrabrook Marriage *Barbara Hannay*	1814	0 263 18594 X

HISTORICAL ROMANCE™

The Earl and the Pickpocket *Helen Dickson*		
	310	0 263 18509 5
A Knight of Honour *Anne Herries*	311	0 263 18510 9
Saving Sarah *Gail Ranstrom*	312	0 263 18956 2

MEDICAL ROMANCE™

The Doctor's Rescue Mission *Marion Lennox*		
	577	0 263 18479 X
The Latin Surgeon *Laura MacDonald*	578	0 263 18480 3
Dr Cusack's Secret Son *Lucy Clark*	579	0 263 18481 1
Her Surgeon Boss *Abigail Gordon*	580	0 263 18482 X

0905 Gen Std LP

MILLS & BOON®

Live the emotion

NOVEMBER 2005 HARDBACK TITLES

ROMANCE™

The Sheikh's Innocent Bride *Lynne Graham*		
	H6276	0 263 18771 3
Bought by the Greek Tycoon *Jacqueline Baird*		
	H6277	0 263 18772 1
The Count's Blackmail Bargain *Sara Craven*	H6278	0 263 18773 X
The Italian Millionaire's Virgin Wife *Diana Hamilton*		
	H6279	0 263 18774 8
A Ruthless Agreement *Helen Brooks*	H6280	0 263 18775 6
The Carides Pregnancy *Kim Lawrence*	H6281	0 263 18776 4
Prince's Love-Child *Carole Mortimer*	H6282	0 263 18777 2
Mistress on Demand *Maggie Cox*	H6283	0 263 18778 0
Her Italian Boss's Agenda *Lucy Gordon*	H6284	0 263 18779 9
A Bride Worth Waiting For *Caroline Anderson*		
	H6285	0 263 18780 2
A Father in the Making *Ally Blake*	H6286	0 263 18781 0
The Wedding Surprise *Trish Wylie*	H6287	0 263 18782 9
Jack and the Princess *Raye Morgan*	H6288	0 263 18783 7
Daddy's Little Memento *Teresa Carpenter*	H6289	0 263 18784 5
Coming Back for His Bride *Abigail Gordon*	H6290	0 263 18785 3
A Perfect Father *Laura Iding*	H6291	0 263 18786 1

HISTORICAL ROMANCE™

The Venetian's Mistress *Ann Elizabeth Cree*		
	H615	0 263 18823 X
Bachelor Duke *Mary Nichols*	H616	0 263 18824 8
The Knave and the Maiden *Blythe Gifford*	H617	0 263 18951 1

MEDICAL ROMANCE™

Her Celebrity Surgeon *Kate Hardy*	M529	0 263 18847 7
The Surgeon's Rescue Mission *Dianne Drake*		
	M530	0 263 18848 5

MILLS & BOON®

Live the emotion

NOVEMBER 2005 LARGE PRINT TITLES

ROMANCE™

Bought: One Bride *Miranda Lee*	1815	0 263 18595 8
His Wedding Ring of Revenge *Julia James*	1816	0 263 18596 6
Blackmailed into Marriage *Lucy Monroe*	1817	0 263 18597 4
The Greek's Forbidden Bride *Cathy Williams*		
	1818	0 263 18598 2
Pregnant: Father Needed *Barbara McMahon*		
	1819	0 263 18599 0
A Nanny for Keeps *Liz Fielding*	1820	0 263 18600 8
The Bridal Chase *Darcy Maguire*	1821	0 263 18601 6
Marriage Lost and Found *Trish Wylie*	1822	0 263 18602 4

HISTORICAL ROMANCE™

The Viscount's Secret *Dorothy Elbury*	313	0 263 18511 7
The Defiant Mistress *Claire Thornton*	314	0 263 18512 5
A Scandalous Proposal *Julia Justiss*	315	0 263 19294 6

MEDICAL ROMANCE™

Her Emergency Knight *Alison Roberts*	581	0 263 18483 8
The Doctor's Fire Rescue *Lilian Darcy*	582	0 263 18484 6
A Very Special Baby *Margaret Barker*	583	0 263 18485 4
The Children's Heart Surgeon *Meredith Webber*		
	584	0 263 18486 2

1005 Gen Std LP